Mark Swallow

Mark Swallow was born in 1963. He wrote his first adult novel, *Teaching Little Fang*, in 1990, following a year of travelling and teaching in China. The book won him a Betty Trask prize. His second adult novel, *Skater*, followed soon after. Since then, he has also travelled and taught in India, and is now teaching in Bristol, where he lives with his wife and young son. He has never dared get 0% in an exam.

The author would like to thank his parents,
Delsey Burns, Will McLoughlin,
Susie Dent, Amanda Stevens,
Jim Honeybone, Ena Macnamara
and Lucy Courtenay
for their help and support.

Mark Swallow

((Collins flamingo

🏰 *An imprint of HarperCollinsPublishers*

First published in Great Britain by Collins 2002

1 3 5 7 9 10 8 6 4 2

Collins is an imprint of HarperCollins*Publishers* Ltd, 77-85 Fulham
Palace Road, Hammersmith, London W6 8JB

The HarperCollins website address is www.**fire**and**water**.com

ISBN 0 00 712649 2

Printed and bound in Great Britain by Omnia Books Limited,
Glasgow G64

Conditions of Sale

for Sarah

TAKE YOUR SEATS...

THIS IS THE LAST GCSE EXAM FOR MOST OF YOU –
FOR MANY, YOUR LAST EXAM EVER. SO LET'S MAKE IT
A SMOOTH ONE, EH? AND LET'S GET THE HATS OFF,
SHALL WE? BRAINS NEED CIRCULATING AIR...

*Laila says she is going to be waiting for me afterwards. I
like thinking of her waiting outside. For me.*

*So why did I try to put her off? Only made her more
interested.*

Why?

*Because I know our school gates. This is where the hard ones
wait, just beyond the civilisation of school – No Sir Land –
beyond the dinksy policies on bullying, lunch queue rules and
keep-left-in-the-corridors. They are the mothers who will
welcome us today, many of them excluded from our year,
excluded from our exams. They are so chuffed with their
exchange of the acned playground tarmac for the hard lines of
the pavement. And they will have brought their friends, kids of
much more experience, almost certainly kids of some substance.*

As a junior I used to creep past with my mates, thrilling at their palm-held electronics, their leisure wear and their trainers. Their occasional cars higgled and piggled against the kerb, bucking with the bassiest tunes. Their tangle of getaway bikes, small enough to ride through a copper's legs. I admit to being impressed once but I'd sooner hop over the back fence these days.

At the end of this last GCSE I will leave this school, these peers. I'll say goodbye to a few, see you later to even fewer, and nothing to most. I won't bother to diss a peer – just disappear out the back and loop round past the garage to see if Laila really has come for me.

I SAID HATS OFF! AND THERE SHOULD BE NO MOBILES IN THE HALL.

The kids who have tried to keep their caps on are now being told to remove them before we can start. The only progress that's been made in a generation's fight against school uniform – and just when they let us off wearing them, we want caps after all.

RIGHT, ARE YOU ALL READY?

Now, are we all ready? The invigilator invites us to start, so let us begin.

The best place to start is on the stairs at home where we used to spend a lot of time sitting. Always the same formation, my little sister on the top one and Tommy on the second, with me down a couple and leaning against the wall. Our legs had habits too. Rosie bunched hers under her chin, Tommy's were all over the place, never still, while mine pointed down the stairs with the right foot on top of the left trying to line itself up with the bottom of the hand rail. This is how we used to sit – for the clicking of the Christmas photograph, for the looking at ourselves in the mirror above the stairs and for the listening in on the grown-ups.

The photographs are still an easy present for Mum to give lucky friends and relations each year. We used to spend hours finessing our poses in the mirror but our ears were always on the kitchen where we might just be being talked about by Mum and Dad.

Five years ago I was the hot topic. I have been discussed a lot since but it was five years ago, when I was about to leave primary school, that I first picked up some interesting stuff.

My 'educational destination' was still undecided. Dad was finally losing what had been a long and cold war to send me to a private school rather than the local comprehensive. Still he refused to believe Mum would not change her mind at some point. She was furious he would not just roll over and accept her passionate belief in the importance of supporting state schools "with our own flesh and blood". But even she was not as cross as Rosie and Tommy, who had nothing else to listen in on for weeks.

Dad worked very hard in a bank. He still does, in the City of London. Apparently that is the main reason we were able to afford this house, the biggest on Rockenden Road and just in either Hounslow or Isleworth depending on how you look at it. He travels all over the world so doesn't mind being close to Heathrow. Mum has lived in the area all her life and works as a secretary at the health centre.

And how did I feel? I didn't like the idea of leaving my mates, who were going to Chevy Oak Comprehensive. But I didn't like the idea of disappointing Dad either when he had put me up or down or by for a school somewhere else. He kept on about the facilities and class sizes and the paintballing club they ran on Saturday afternoons. Mum seemed to have heard enough of it.

"This is where we live," I heard from my stair. "It may not be particularly peaceful or lovely, Martin, but we are here in a neighbourhood – yes, *neighbourhood* – we know and in which we are *known*. And Jack, as one of our children, lives here too."

"I am well aware—"

"The hell you are! This is not some computer package or bloody car we're talking about here. It's Jack's education. You can get excited about your heated wing mirrors waggling for you at the push of a button, about your gleaming veneer and your plush velour, but Jack does not need extras. He needs the local school, solid, sane and free."

"It's got nothing to do with cars, Polly."

"What are these posh schools of yours if not shiny cars with tinted windows which purr shut on the smog? You can go paintballing whenever you like but leave Jack here with us."

"Very funny. A few months from now you'll be sorry for this, Polly."

"You want him schooled, Martin, and I want him educated. It's as simple as that. Heir-conditioning with an aitch! That's what you're after."

Our teacher at Primary was our friend. The floor of our form room was thick with rugs and cushions. The walls were beautifully decorated by all of us. I used to think that's why they were called primary colours. There were amazing displays by our teacher with her perfect handwriting which I longed to copy completely perfectly. How could anyone (except Razza who has always had Special Needs) hate reading in our Cosy Corner? There was so much friendship in that room we even had loads to spare for the slimy lizards in their tank. There wasn't even a bell. Instead, at the end of break, a toddler would proudly brandish that sign, 'Please walk in now showing care and respect to everyone in are school'.

But Dad's descriptions of secondary classrooms, delivered in chilling detail when he tucked me in at the end of the day, reminded me of Mexican Indian arenas we'd done in comparative civilisation where they played football with prisoners' heads and volleyball with freshly ripped-out hearts.

On his way back to the office from Moscow, he invited me out to lunch in my last primary school half-term. I went along a little nervously. We sat in the window of a posh place in Richmond and Dad, in a grand mood, ordered caviar.

"I'd like to introduce you to an expensive habit of mine," he said when it arrived. "Mum doesn't like it, of course..."

"Caviar – or you eating it?"

"Either, Jack." He spooned the shiny black stuff on to some fancy toast. "Would you like to try it?" For each go he pouted his lips like a gibbon to make sure he didn't drop any.

"Eeeerrr! No, thanks, Dad." I gobbled at my melon.

"Go on!"

The caviar did look quite beautiful, like a load of full stops.

"Naaah, Dad!"

"I won't offer often, Jack!"

So I craned forward and took a nibble from the toast he held. It tasted sensational. All my buds were up and quivering and demanding more.

"Steady," said Dad, snaffling the last of it himself. "But, I tell you what – last a couple of years at this comp, establish yourself as a survivor – and then I'll stop banging on about different sorts of schools."

"I'll try, Dad."

"And if you hate it after two years, we'll try somewhere else. Either way we'll celebrate with some more of this black stuff!"

When his phone rang all this rare enjoyment

drained from his face. He said he had been "summoned". I said I'd take the bus, expecting him to tell me I was too young and that he would give me a lift. But he didn't seem to know I was too young, so I did it. No bother.

My mates Michael, Razza and a few others who had come up to Chevy Oak together were sitting on some steps in the playground, fresh young bums on worn-out bricks, discussing the planes which were even louder and lower here than at Primary. One of Heathrow's smaller runways was actually visible, its huge grass safety zone separated from our playground by a high wire fence.

Razza started cussing another kid, just having a little laugh, casting around to see who couldn't take it, eventually suggesting that this boy's mum had "shagged a camel". I was wondering why dads never got cussed when Michael stole Razza's line.

"And the camel died of shame."

The kid was blasted away by our laughter straight into Mr Ronaldson, our form tutor. He looked at us each in turn and then pointed to some letters engraved on the vertical of the step beside me.

"See what that says, lads?"

I could make out the name 'Dennis' and, also, 'wanks'.

"The longest piece of writing Denny did during his five years here," Ronaldson went on. "Do you know what he used to do in lessons?"

"No, sir."

"He used to giggle, Jack. At first the kids laughed with him, but soon they got bored of Denny and began to ignore him. He began giggling louder, every term louder and louder. But do you know what? He left without a single GCSE." He looked at each of us again. "Remember Denny, won't you?"

"Yes, sir," we said and I shifted uncomfortably to cover the name and the verb.

"He's only me uncle," said Michael, suddenly.

Ronaldson wasn't thrown. "Well, you ask him about his time here, Michael. See if he hasn't got any tips for you."

"He had a laugh, though," said Michael. A plane was overhead. "Denny had a good time, he did."

Ronaldson had moved away but he turned and looked steadily at Michael, who tried to keep chuckling. "Isn't laughing now, is he, Michael?"

Although I had no plans to giggle my way through the curriculum, I was not so interested in the classroom. I needed to show Dad I could hack the other parts: the corridors, the landings and the playground. I had no fear of being a loser on the Denny scale. But in what way was I going to be a winner? Certainly not by sitting on these steps waiting to be kicked. My parents' voices were still loud in my head despite the planes.

"He's a sensitive kid."

"It's a sensitive school."

"We should be exercising our right – our ability – to choose the best school for him."

"We are. This is *the best school, Martin."*

There were groups of older boys before me now, too cool to move. They didn't even bother trying to impress the girls in their cropped uniforms, skirts rolled up to the hilt, who coped just as coolly with the disappointment. Softer-looking kids hunkered down in corners and took it out on small insects and old birds while groups of little girls promenaded the perimeter, shouting, pouting, spouting.

But this playground was really about boys chasing footballs, knees punching the air violently, feet slapping on the tarmac. There was so much shouting of the one word "Fuck!" in so many different forms and tones that it was almost a one-word language. Most of all, there was so much fucking football.

As another plane came over we saw a massive shot

beat a goalkeeper and then whack a tiny Year Seven, the camel-shagger's son, on the rebound. We could see his soundless shriek but none of us moved. There were so many other games going on that people were being taken out all the time, so many bursts of speed and screeching halts. A boy pulled up his shirt after scoring and did a flip in front of jeering girls. We still had seven minutes to survive and my cherry drink was backing up on me. This was no place to relax but still there seemed no way off the step.

Two more huge people chasing a ball clashed heads right by us.

"Fucking tosser."

"Fuck, man!"

They squared up to each other but decided they had each kept enough respect so they shoulder-barged each other and parted with a friendly "Fuck you!"

"Fuck that must of hurt," whispered Razza with admiration, smacking his own head.

"Like fuck." Michael was lapping it up, and indicated with his head that a fellow new kid was hiding a football under his jacket. With three minutes of break to go he grabbed it off him and they all stood up to try and play in a little space near the steps.

"Come on, Jack, mate!"

Hating fucking football, I stood reluctantly. It was a way off the steps but I felt like a shaky lamb out for the first gambol. When the ball came to me it passed right through my legs and into one of the huddles of seniors. It was lazily scooped up. The last moments of break were bounced away by our ball in huge hands. Then as the buzzer sounded this kid, a stubby pony-tail drongo, booted it to the far end of the playground where another brute bicycle-kicked it on the volley way up over the fence into airport territory.

"Cheers, Jack," said Michael. As if it was his ball anyway. Stacey Timms and her little posse, who'd come up from our Primary at the same time, called me a "prat" in passing. The ball's owner looked at me miserably. I looked back as the playground emptied. Gulls wheeled down to feast on our litter and I realised I hadn't eaten the cheesy strings Mum had packed for me. Tears queued in my ducts but somehow I blocked them out.

From here we went into whole school assembly – my first visit to this hall in which I am sitting now – to be addressed by Bumcheeks, the headteacher.

"As you know," he began after many minutes of staff shushing, "Chevy Oak is one of the most popular schools in the borough and I would like to start this morning –

this academic year – by simply congratulating you on being here."

Older kids back-slapped each other facetiously.

"Our greatly improved set of results last year is still more evidence of a school on the move, a school aiming high, a school marching forward with confidence."

At which point everyone began stamping in time, which caused Bumcheeks to turn bright red and pause a while.

"There are, it must be said, more of you than ever before. We are jam-packed in here, jam-packed in our very narrow corridors and in the playground even more jam-packed since the marvellous new block has gone up. We cannot reduce your size because, boys and girls, you have a habit of growing like aubergines. From now on, as you will have noticed from the new signs, you will keep left in the corridors and observe the new queuing system at lunch. But the main measure I wish to introduce – from tomorrow – has just been further justified by yet another nasty incident in the playground, a Year Seven boy hit in the face by a—"

The chortling briefly drowned him.

"Listen! Hit in the face by a football. Therefore I have decided on a measure we have long been considering – a ban on full-size footballs in the playground. From tomorrow you will only be allowed to use..."

"Wot?" The need to listen was suddenly urgent.

"I will tell you what just as soon as I get silence..."

"Oh WOT!"

"... only be allowed to use tennis balls."

The baying began in earnest.

"Nah, nah, nah!"

"You can't do that, Bumcheeks."

Chairs bucked noisily.

"Tight, man. That's dark."

Aiming high, I looked up to check no sunbeam from an upper window was singling me out for warm favour. Three hours in school and the dreaded football outlawed!

The atmosphere was dangerous for the rest of the day as kids made especially violent use of their footballs before the ban. In a similar spirit of urgent frustration two older boys slammed me up against some lockers so a padlock dug into my back. Then they jabbed something else up into my heart. So much for sunbeams. Was this the "recreational bullying" Dad had told me to watch out for?

"Take this one for example," said one to the other as if continuing a debate. "There's a bunch of nasty little stiffs coming into this school. Why's there not room for footballs? Let me tellya. Because of this."

"You are in fact a stiff," said the other who'd nicked our football.

"So neat in his new school uniform."

"Neat as mumsy fuck." His pony-tail quivered with anger.

"You want to loosen up a little, mate." He yanked my tie and then, on second thoughts, tightened it totally. The other stabbed me again – this time right up into the armpit – and then scored me across the forehead with the same weapon.

"Record-keeping's important. We got so many to get through we don't want to be repeating ourselfs, innit."

Michael saw us from the far end of the corridor and shouted to me that he was going to get his Uncle Denny to handle it after school.

"Nah, actually I'll get him. He'll come straight up school!" They turned towards Michael on his mobile and must have clocked the genetic link because they swore and dropped me over a fire extinguisher to hurry off in the opposite direction. Michael pulled me out of the corridor and into a classroom where he loosened my tie.

"Is it blood?" I asked, raising my head from my hands, gasping.

"Could be, man. Just in time, eh?" He was triumphant, breathing hard and fast, rabbit-punching the whiteboard and then plunging his face into a bag of crisps he'd ripped apart.

"Thanks for your help, mate." I was still shaking and dabbing at my wound, which was in fact pink highlighter pen.

"It was nothing. Do you want me to take you somewhere? To Ronaldson? I'd like to tell him what made them run. Teach him to diss our Denny!"

"Nah, I'm fine..." But nor did I want to be left to face these corridors alone.

Dad came in late from Zürich, but there was enough time for him to get furious on my behalf. Tommy and Rosie didn't even bother to take up their stair positions but I settled with some nervousness.

"Do you see now, Polly?"

"See what?" But she had caught a glimpse.

"Jack can't cope. They are beasts in that school. They may be part of your blessed community but that hardly makes it better. They will beat up our son because of the way he looks. He is powerless. What can he do?"

"What did you do at your precious public school, Martin? How did you survive?"

"This didn't happen, if that's what you mean."

"I don't believe *you* weren't bullied."

"Don't say it like that. I wasn't terrorised. This Chevy Oak is an aggressive place. His primary school cardboard castles and peppermint creams, they won't help him now. Football might have done but he seems to play that less and less."

I shot downstairs and burst in. "I gave it up today!" They barely looked at me.

"So what, Martin? Games aren't everything." Mum was plunging her needle in and out of my blazer.

"Football isn't a game. It's a vital early form of communication. Before they can really talk, boys kick a ball. And if boy doesn't kick ball, boy gets himself kicked. It's body language at its simplest."

Mum turned on me.

"Why *don't* you play?"

Stay strong, Mum, I remember thinking. You don't have to ask his questions for him. They both looked at me.

"It goes through my legs, especially at this new school. We have to play with tennis balls."

"Tennis ball football?" cried Dad. "Now I've heard it all."

My first break at Chevy Oak School had broken painfully. The second had to be much, much better. These twenty minutes, I could see, were the day's key jostle time – preen-time, be-seen-time – even more important than the end of school at the front gate.

It poured with rain lesson three. Bumcheeks came on the loudspeaker to say we could spend break in our classrooms. I was relieved. But the sun mocked me, coming out brilliantly just before the buzzer, and I was soon being urged towards the sopping tarmac by hundreds of kids.

The airport was as busy as usual, executive jets from the side runway taking off directly across the playground. Would Dad actually be able to look down on my antics? The sudden sun warmed me a bit through the reinforced seams of my blazer. Lots of juniors were enjoying the new football rule, and even Michael and Razza were mincing about with tennis balls. Nothing there for me of course. I remained on the step, alone with the voices.

"*This is where we live,*" I could hear Mum say. "*It may not be particularly peaceful or lovely, Martin, but...*" I traced her sing-song tone with my finger on the pitted brickwork.

Two of our classmates were taking the opportunity to play mini-tennis with a couple of old racquets. I saw my pony-tailed attacker from yesterday casually interrupt the mini-tennis ("Can I be ball boy, children?") and walk off with their ball to laugh coldly with his mates.

"*He'll be dragged down...*" Dad's insistence was loud inside my head.

"*It's a perfectly good school with a nice mix of all sorts. There aren't that many difficult kids. Besides, what do you think he is going to be dragged down into? This is where he lives – he's in it already. Difficult kids are part of the experience. They lead difficult, realistic lives.*"

"*And they tend to become very difficult adolescents. Difficult men.*"

"*All schools produce difficult men – all schools. Jack will learn to cope. He's got so much going on here. He doesn't need to go whizzing off. He can learn to whiz here.*"

"*He's sensitive. He'll be bullied.*"

"*And he won't be bullied somewhere else?*"

"Bullied in the wrong way."

Suddenly I was standing, with what Razza was to describe later as "summat shining in your eye". My legs were no longer lamb-like. It was coiled-spring time.

I grabbed a racquet and fired myself towards the older boys. Half a mile away a Lear jet was accelerating at us, forcing its noise towards the playground.

"Where you going?" Michael barked.

Ducking into the group of older boys, I snatched back the tennis ball from the bully and barged out through the other side. The roar of the plane did little to drown out "You little fuck!" and "Shit, back here now!" but I was running, running towards the fence and everyone in the playground was looking at me. I had just seconds before the plane took off and before I would be brought down, pulled off the chicken wire like a convict.

When I fancied I could see the olive in Dad's Martini, I slid to a stop, swung the racquet and, with champagne timing, crashed the balding sphere into space. As we all watched it go I caught the look of amazement, crinkling into fury, on the pilot's speeding face. The whites of his eyes lit up for an astonished moment as the ball hit his shiny jet.

"Right between the wheels," yelled Michael, skidding to my side with a bunch of new admirers. "Wot a shot!"

They grabbed their groins and danced in mock agony, pretending to be nutted jets.

"Aim high!" I shouted. "Forget your fucking football and aim high!"

The sphere returned to planet Earth to be caught by a laughing senior. More and more kids were doing the groin dance now and pecking their heads up into the air. I began to laugh. If I had really, really caught the Lear between the legs, Dad might have felt the tremor too. Had I made him sit up and take note of me already?

Anything seemed possible during this Lucky Break when the kids of Chevy Oak first looked up from their dribbling. Everyone was congratulating me and cussing pony-tail.

"You was shown!"

"Little kid told you, man," said another. "That was bad!"

He staggered off and I was swamped.

As they hammered my back I smiled. I couldn't help hearing Dad's warning.

"In two years' time Jack will be a basket case, bullied to a jelly."

"Shut up, Martin."

Shut up the pair of you! Just let me enjoy it!

"I will shut up – in a minute. Because if my prediction is true – when it becomes true – I as his father demand the right to send Jack, our by now gelatinous and quivering son, to a fee-paying school."

"After two years he will be even more a part of this area than he is already. He will be two years stronger, Martin. He will have confidence which cannot be bought and no 'rights' of yours are going to mess that up..."

No-one was in at home but Ronaldson rang to confirm that I would have an enormous detention on Friday. I accepted.

"It's not an invitation, Jack."

"Then you can expect me, sir."

Next day I felt I should go back into the playground. But what more could I add to my mantra of yesterday, "Aim high"? Of course every cupboard under every stair had been done over, everyone was brandishing a racquet, squash, badminton, anything – and everyone was scouring the airways. Eventually a jet approached. I was going to give the order – the least I could do – but they all fired far too early. Birds were winded but the plane escaped and hundreds of tennis balls landed in airport territory. Security's Alsatians were soon happily collecting them from the lush grass. More teachers appeared from the school building and they shouted out punishments. I was about the only kid without a racquet.

My jet strike has passed into legend. The day they looked up from their football at the big, wide sky and saw me hit something huge. I was established at Chevy Oak before most of my year group knew the way to the toilets. Jumbo Curling before I had a single pube.

Razza also earned himself a seat at that fashionable first detention. Keen on calling up the emergency services at Primary, he had rung the airport to ask if we could have our balls back – and given his name.

"Detention in your first week, Jack," said Dad, back from Hong Kong.

"Yup."

" What did you get it for?"

I explained. He said he did sometimes take a Martini but was never likely to fly in a Lear jet.

"You seem to be making your mark, eh, Jack?"

"Oh Martin, please! Stay out of his education if you're going to be like that. Imagine what it was like for me dealing with the tutor – and a phone call from the Head."

"At least you aren't having to sew him up again, Polly."

They both ruffled different sides of my head, which was quite big enough for them not to have to mingle fingers. What a good moment, I thought, to put Grandad's clicker to use. This was the only material object he had handed down after a career on the trains and Dad had passed it straight on to me.

I saw a chance to use this device, with which Grandad had counted many thousands of rail travellers during his ticket-collecting days, to provide my banker of a Dad with some statistics, some hard evidence (to back up my permanent grin) of what a good time I was having.

Kids I didn't even know greeted me at the end of Rockenden Road. I notched up seven clicks on my way into school. Others competed for my attention in the corridors and on the stairs. Everywhere it was "Safe, Jack, safe."

"Sweet as a nut, Jumbo."

"You're a chief!"

"Jack's lush an' all!"

Click, click, click.

But how safe did I feel, how sweet was my nut, how lush my chiefiness? The day would show me. The day would show Dad. Statistics.

By break I was up to 157. What with corridor greetings, friendly cussings and happy exchanges during afternoon Maths when a cover teacher tried to control us with her skirt still tucked into her pants, I was pushing 500 clicks by the end of the day. Click, click, click. Safe, Jumbo Jack, safe mate, lush and wicked.

Dad was with us for supper as I explained the study.

"He's enjoying himself, isn't he, Martin?"

"Four hundred and ninety two clicks today, Dad."

"Don't spread yourself too thinly." But I could tell he was pretty pleased. "Establish yourself soundly, remember?" he added. "Build up your defences."

"Listen to the warlord," Mum laughed.

"Dad's a chief, Mum."

"He's listening to me all right, Polly..." said Dad.

But when I went back in to tell them I'd also found 42 text messages on my mobile, they were getting at each other again.

I now needed a woman. Rather than pick a peer I chose Miss Price, our young French teacher. With a word to one or two key players, I ensured that our first few lessons went well. Even Michael shut up for me.

"Jack Curling," she said after a fortnight of progress in our mixed ability set, "you are a good man to go into the jungle with."

"And you are a superb teacher, miss," I groundlessly confided. "It is such a romantic tongue, la langue Français."

I fell in love with her, ignored all other subjects and called her "maman" twice by mistake. And, Mum, I'm afraid her perfume was the first I ever noticed.

Meanwhile I decided to investigate other areas of the school, now that I had conquered the playground. Past the chilly pong and wild noises of the toilets I went, past the bins where gulls fought pigeons for the canteen's old buns, and up past the crazy, clanging music rooms. I was wondering whether there might be opportunities for further self-establishment – in the school library.

It turned out to be a large room full of stiffs and girls clustered at tables or pecking at high walls of shelves with dog-eared signs on: 'Kwikreads!', 'Lotsa Laughs!!' and 'Horror!!!' The main window looked out over the playground and up Jumbo Jack's Runway beyond. I pressed my nose against the glass. I swung my bag up to the sky. I fucking loved this school.

A throat cleared. I turned to see a small dark-haired man behind the desk.

"In the bag drop, please," he said from out of a small head with a nose tipped like Concorde.

"Sorry, sir."

He followed me and my bag to the drop to inform me that he was not a 'sir'.

"I'm not paid as much as a sir so I don't see why I should be sirred. I am Mr Schuman, the Librarian." He stuck out his hand. "And you are?"

Watching your snout, Mister.

"Jack Curling." We shook. (Don't touch teachers but Support Staff's all right.)

"I thought so."

"You know me?"

A plane went overhead.

"I happened to be looking out of the window that day. A remarkable shot. I've been wanting to outlaw aeroplanes for years."

"Really?"

"Approximately every three minutes I yearn for a ban on the beastly birds."

"Well, I was lucky."

"I imagine you suffered."

"What?"

"They went for you, I suppose."

"Yes, but only after I had made my point, Mr Schuman."

He looked at me and smiled.

"Welcome to the library anyway. Do you, by any extraordinary chance, like reading?"

"Not much."

"Something?"

"Adventure?" I hazarded.

He looked disappointed but showed me to the relevant shelf. Much more to my interest was the number of teachers who entered the library, nodded at Schuman and then disappeared into a side room. This struck me as intriguing. I sidled over and Schuman followed.

"They've put me in charge of reprographics as well."

"What's that?"

He threw open the door to reveal a teacher about to kick the side of a large photocopier.

"Of course they don't pay me any extra. I don't complain because I haven't a clue how it works – any more than he has!"

I wasn't sure yet how I would make use of the library but I liked what I'd seen already. The buzzer sounded. Another jumbo wheeled off left as I headed to the next lesson.

Others flourished in different spheres. Michael scored an early success when the Music teacher gave him an hour, for gobbing into Razza's cornet during 'orchestra'.

"A hour? A hour? You can't do that!"

"I can," he said, uneasy with the challenge.

"Not without twenty-four hours' notice you can't. What if I'm not home when I'm expected? Eh?"

Michael has always been good on his rights and others' wrongs.

"Your mother will be relieved."

This teacher couldn't even do sarcasm.

"Nah, nah, nah, that ain't funny. You can't do it, mister. Twenty minutes, innit, twenty minutes max or Denny'll come and explain matters t'ya."

There were other coups. Stacey Timms claimed to have done it in the toilets with a Year Nine protected by a salt and vinegar crisp bag. Razza, the son of the caretaker, told a teacher to kiss his arse. Clearly I was needed to raise the tone.

····

The following week the school secretary came to pull me out of a lively Music lesson.

"Sorry to, er, interrupt – but could I borrow Jack for a moment? There's a visitor for him."

I didn't know what model I had demanded: anything so long as she was drop-head gorgeous and red. I wasn't disappointed and, if my man was, he didn't show it.

"Don't worry, sir. You did write a remarkably good letter. Fooled us fair and square. This is the least we can do – and perhaps in a few years' time our indulgence will pay off in terms of brand loyalty. The horn is in the usual place. One blast should do the trick."

I climbed inside to hit the horn, which made such a very horny sound that the music-room windows filled with kids – and other windows too. After smearing the mahogany veneer with my sticky fingers, I got slowly back out, pacing around her and leaning into gales of envy. I shot a few questions at the man, cocking my head in interest at his replies. I took the odd note in my homework diary before languidly checking my phone for messages: too many to cope with now. Might have to get a school secretary myself.

I eased back inside and, to grateful cheers, sent the roof up and back, retracting sexily into its slot. I nodded to the school's façade which now included a lifelike bust of Bumcheeks. The bust sprouted a quick finger and bellowed, "My study, now!"

"I have meant to make your acquaintance earlier, young man. Of course I have spoken to your mother once or twice. I spent a good deal of time at the start of the year apologising for you to the airport authority and now I dare say a car manufacturer will be in touch. This is not going to become a craze, do you understand?"

"Yes sir." I knew Razza had written to a Chinese company about a clever-looking military vehicle which could fire bridges across raging rivers.

"And I think you would do well from now on to restrict your activities to the school. Stop getting muddled up with the outside world."

"You mean *lower* my horizons, sir? I have always tried to aim high..."

"I mean, Jack Curling, focus your energies where they count, which is in the classroom."

Before taking this advice, I couldn't resist writing to the photocopier company and getting a manual which I learnt off by heart. Schuman was much impressed by my enlarging, my stapling and my shrinking. He gave me increasing access to what I now saw as key school power node.

"I've never really understood any of the buttons but you seem to realise it has been underachieving," he moaned. "Like so much round here..."

There were delicious dividends. Teachers, stressed and confused, so often left behind on the glass what they had been copying. Salary statements, pages of their own boring stories, an invitation to a taster bell-ringing evening in Feltham. Nothing, however, on Miss Price, whom I was looking forward to introducing to Mum and Dad at parents' evening.

The atmosphere was good. The teachers looked a bit knackered but the really mad kids never come to these dos, their madder folks refusing to be bollocked by smarmy young graduates – so there was little for anyone to worry about on such a beautiful sunny evening.

I had left Miss Price to last on the bookings sheet. I told Mum even as I saw the Science teacher setting out his table that he had said he was unable to make it.

"Family matters, I think."

This avoided a difficult meeting for me and gave Dad the chance to moan about the school ("We've come all this way and he can't be bothered to stay. Think of the holidays they all get...") which improved his mood. History, Maths, English and ICT passed OK except Mum thought the English teacher was a bit snobby.

"Always were," said Dad.

Bumcheeks breezed by and greeted us civilly which did no harm. Ronaldson let me down a little by saying I wasn't trying hard enough and called me a "great asset", which sounded rude. Miss Price alone remained, in the still sunny Modern Languages room.

"Hello, miss," I beamed at her, eagerly pulling up a chair and letting Mum and Dad find their own. "How are you?"

"Fine, thank you, Jack. Hello, Mr Curling, Mrs Curling." She'd done her research and knew there were no carers, guardians or steps for me.

"Really, I have nothing but praise for Jack. He has been a wonderful student all year and he has improved a great deal."

"In what way, Miss Price? Can you give us some specifics?"

She looked at Dad and entered into some curriculum detail and the way I'd been handling it.

"... Furthermore he has also been a tremendous help to other less talented students in class, especially in group work. He's even helped with some of their homework."

"I can't see what good can come of that," sniffed Dad. "That was called plain cheating in my day."

But he and I both knew Mum would love it. She squeezed my shoulder.

"It's really nice to hear about you helping – poor Michael, was it?"

I remembered my cheeky little comments in his margins, 'Bon soir, Madame, je suis partout!' and 'Ici aussi!' and I beamed too.

On the way to the car, Dad put his arm lightly round me and said, "Well, they seem to like you, Jack."

"Yeah, it's all right there, isn't it, Dad?"

"Your tutor is a funny looking man though."

"Oh I do like Mr Ronaldson!" chimed Mum. "He's got such a nice way with you all. And he really does care."

"Yes, Mum, I suppose he does."

"Oh definitely, Jack. You are lucky to have him."

I asked her quietly the meaning of 'asset' and she didn't hear.

"No, Martin, we'll walk thank you."

"I came across a stall trying to sell the Business

Studies department, Jack," said Dad as he unlocked the car. "Very enthusiastic teacher actually. You might like to find out some more about that..."

"Jack seems to be doing the business anyway, don't you think, Martin?" Mum hugged me and laughed. Suddenly I wished I were alone with Dad again, eating caviar and hearing about how he really thought I was doing on the survival front.

He drove home, and Mum and I meandered back past the familiar premises of Nobbi, our neighbourhood greengrocer, who was just throwing down his metal casements.

"How's it going, with big school?" he called.

"Fine thanks, Nob."

"One to be proud of, eh, Mrs C?"

Mum laughed and patted my head.

"I really am proud of you," she said as we walked on. "You've settled in so brilliantly. Even Dad has to admit it."

"Do you think he does? Thanks. Did you like Miss Price?"

"Well she certainly seems to like you."

"Do you think so?"

"Nice girl. Horrid perfume though."

It sometimes seemed to me that the school tried to

lay on events to distract us from our work. How else can you interpret the arrival of student teachers? Certainly it is open season if you're lucky enough to get one. Which we were – in place of the History teacher. Clean-cut and youthful, Mr Carew was very friendly. So we took the piss immediately.

"How long are you with us, Mr Car*oooo*?" I felt obliged to open the hostilities.

"Oh, for a good long while. You must think of me as your permanent teacher now, Jake."

"It's Jack actually."

"Sorry."

"That's all right, Mr Car*oooo*, but don't you return to the institute soon – for feedback? Stress counselling?"

"What? Look, why don't you just get on with the task?"

"Only if you tell us your Aims for the lesson."

"My aims?"

"And afterwards your Objectives. They should be written in your lesson plan."

"You cheeky little—"

"In fact, Mr Car*oooo*, I wouldn't half mind seeing your entire Scheme of Work. Michael's Uncle Denny takes a lively interest in modern approaches to the subject, when he's not pumping iron down at the gym..."

This got reported to Bumcheeks, who gave me a

two-hour though he could hardly deny I'd been concentrating my energies in the classroom – and specifically on the teacher.

The next few History lessons went better – from Carew's point of view – largely because the Head himself was 'observing'. Nevertheless, Razza couldn't resist again asking our trainee when he was going to let our 'proper' teacher back in and soon there was a general chorus of "How do you do, Mr Car*oooo*?" going down.

In the photocopy room one lunchtime Miss Price said Mr Carew was having a tough time with some of his classes.

"Does he teach you, Jack?"

"Er…"

"Well, if you do come across him just be helpful – as I know you can be."

"How do you mean?"

"It's a bit of a jungle, as we know. And his supervisor's in next week."

"Leave it with me, miss," I said, flattered to have her go so unprofessional on me. "We'll get Mr Carew through."

Just for *yoooou*.

But here I made two fatal underestimations: of my

classmates' malice and of Carew's teaching skills. For the lesson in question, with the geezer from the institute stroking his clipboard at the back of the room, Carew made a pig of a choice. Of course he had worked it down to the last minute. I could see the spindly writing of his lesson plan had dedicated the eleventh and the twelfth minute after ten to 'greeting pupils and settling them'. He did the first and I just about managed the second though Michael, it so happened, was out for blood today.

"Fuck off, Jack," he said, as I tried to hush him. When I gestured to the back of the class he elaborately turned in his chair and whistled salaciously at the grey-haired suit already scribbling on to his clipboard. We wet ourselves. Had to.

"Right, everyone," Mr Carew started, "today we've got a lot to get through so I just want to explain a few things and then we'll, er, get right into the fun stuff. OK?"

"We know you, Mr Car*oooo*!" had started up, though it mutated around Michael's area into, "We'll have you, Mr Car*oooo*!"

I had to break the destructive cycle – for Miss Price's sake.

"Sir?"

"Yes, what is it, Jack?" He was wary.

"Can I just say something before the, er, fun stuff?"

"As long as it's relevant. And quick." He looked at his watch and I realised I was eating into his three minutes' introduction so I just blurted it out.

"Can I just say I've never really seen the point of History..."

"What?"

"Up till now, I mean. Until *you* started taking us. You make it come alive. I think a lot of us feel the same way..."

I was just trying to help. But this was not the way to do it. Mr Carew smiled with gratitude for about a second but then the peers started burrowing noses into imaginary holes and making powerful sucking noises which darkened his brow.

"Let's talk about your love for the subject *after* the lesson, shall we?" He then revealed his absurd plans for cutting out statements about Napoleon's life, discarding the false ones and ordering the trues chronologically. On sugar paper, if you please. With scissors. And glue.

I tried to cheat the historical inevitability of Mr Carew turning to another profession. I still ask for forgiveness from time to time. Mr Car*oooo*, I did try but you were one of my failures, a campaign too far.

He was everywhere – and nowhere – that lesson. I

still like Napoleon and firmly believe we should have buried him as he fancied in Westminster Abbey. He taught us a thing or two. Mr Carew, however, didn't. And when, towards the end of that deciding battle he set about retrieving the weapons, seven pairs of scissors and seven glue sticks, he only got six scissors – and no glues.

"Come on, can we have the rest of the gear in? Quickly, shall we?"

Nothing more came forth. So Mr Carew panicked and shouted at us more desperately.

"Right! Open your bags! Come on! Everyone! Now! Open them!"

He moved through the desks, abusing our privacy with the bag search. Car*oooo*, Car*oooo*, now nothing can save you! Even quite harmless punters glared at him as he approached their bags with his rummaging adult touch. We don't touch you, you don't touch us. Or our bags. Ever.

"Don't come any closer," said Michael, his voice rich with warning.

"Come on then. Let's see what you've got in there, Michael."

Michael drew out his mobile and put it slowly on the desk.

"What else have you got? Come on..."

Another mobile. Laughter. And another and another. More and more, louder laughter. Michael stared at him as he put each one down on the desk.

"All right, all right, that's *enough*. I won't ask you how you come to have these in your bag." But Michael, still staring, pulled out another three to massive approval.

"Stop it, stop it! What about the glue?"

Mr Carew backed away in despair. I raised my eyes to the ceiling where I knew they'd have been fired and his sad eyes came with me. There, that's what you get for your practical History, seven stalactiting glue sticks.

The buzzer began and everyone had charged out of the door before the final clang.

"Car*ooo*, Car*ooo*, you're through, you're through!"

Mr Carew's head was in his hands so he didn't see Razza toss the missing pair of scissors into the bin and he didn't see me shrug helplessly at his supervisor who was drawing a line across his clipboard, through Mr Carew.

So, now I had conquered the playground and the photocopier. The corridors held no fears and I could handle most things in a classroom, excepting incompetent student teachers. Furthermore I had an ongoing relationship with a qualified teacher. But I wasn't finished yet. I wanted to learn more about the staffroom. Razza's account of trying to get into this sacred space in order to find a teacher during break had made a great impression on us all.

"They just screamed they did, screamed at me to get outside."

"Who did?" we asked.

"Loads, all going 'Get out!'. I felt like I was blasted back into the corridor."

"What d'ya do?" we went.

"Course I wasn't having that, specially being as my dad's caretaker, I mean site supervisor, and they never made him feel all right in there neither. So once I'd recovered me senses I goes right back in."

"And...?"

"That Physics teacher only body-checked me! I swear he did. An' he's built, man. He goes, 'You are never, ever, allowed to come in here. Do you follow?'"

"Didja?" we went.

"I went, 'I follow. I hear what you say. But it ain't right. Sir.'"

"What did he go?"

"Slammed the door in me face, didn't he!"

"Didja tell your dad?"

"Course. But he jus' went, 'Wot you want to went in there for? There's nothing for you in there my son. Nothing for me an' all,' he went."

"But didja get a look in?" we went. "What were they doing in there, the teachers?"

"Sittin', talkin' and with Ms Grundle's buns and cakes bulging down their necks. Mainly they was jus' feastin'."

"So what if you *have* to see one of them in break?"

"Wait outside The Door, innit," said Razza. "Catch 'em on the way in or out."

"Or wait and wait," we went, "and wait and wait and wait, more likely."

"Innit," went Razza. "They ain't in any hurry to serve ya. They've got easy chairs in there an' all."

"Bastards." In this school, chairs upholstered in

anything more than plywood, gob and gum have always been exciting.

"The bastards!" we chorused again. Clearly I had to get in there. Yes, Jack Curling had to do something about the staffroom.

I was leaving for home one afternoon as Miss Price drove out of the gates in her ashtray of a car. Perhaps she could help me with this campaign, I thought, preparing myself to wave and smile with my best side. But there in the passenger seat was Mr Carew, pale-faced, with eyes red and, I noticed, staring straight at me.

"That's him! That's the kid!"

I didn't need to lip-read the words which spattered against the grey interior. The car swerved and I hopped into the border as Miss Price stopped and opened her window.

"Jack?" She looked at her passenger – whose hand she was holding. "Is this really the boy?" She turned her clear, fresh complexion on me again. "I can't believe you're responsible for this. If only you could understand what it is you have done—"

"But, miss—"

"Why do you find it hard to believe?" Mr Carew was snarling. "He's just another fucking teenager."

"Calm down, sweetheart! One day this youngster will be ashamed of himself, one day Jack'll have to take responsibility for this. And to think I once asked for your help, Jack!"

"Please, miss, listen won't you?"

But the window scratched shut and they bumped out into the road, leaving me as crushed as the pansies I was standing on.

Next term's new idea from Bumcheeks, to which he dedicated a lengthy assembly, was Culinary Studies. Equal opportunities for the boys, while the girls go to do 'Motor Vehicle'. He had appointed Mrs Sally Donald, and us lads were soon offering up sincere thanks that her restaurant career had veered in our humble direction. For me personally she filled the gap created by the news (surprise, surprise) that there was now a Mrs Carew. But more than that, Mrs Donald (who insisted on us calling her Sal) won us over with her brilliant lessons. We sat like so many rows of fresh fairy cakes longing for her smiles, which she sprinkled across us in hundreds and thousands. And all because she had cottoned on to a new educational idea that us boys like to be praised.

The Culinary Studies suite was like a busy restaurant kitchen. We were her apprentices and she would threaten one moment to slice us up with her knives and next kiss her fingers in our face, all but hugging us before popping out for a fag on her window ledge. She was not good at hanging on to her cigarettes which kids tended to nick by the bushel from her bulging bag but it was seen to that she never lost her purse or mobile. Bumcheeks was always dropping in on the 'new subject' .

"We can't have you doing nothing in my lessons, honoured Head," she'd say, and before he knew it his bumcheeks would be framed in a little apron and he'd be beating the guts out of an egg.

Ms Grundle, the school catering manager, was a less amused but no less frequent visitor, huffing in to retrieve pans and ladles which Sal had taken from the canteen. It seemed that "Lady Disgruntle", as Sal called her to her face, was an even more embittered member of the support staff than Mr Schuman or Razza's dad.

One morning Sal praised my rock cakes and drew the class's attention to my tray. "They're not perfect, Jack, but they're pretty perfect." She munched into a second, her crumbed and glossy lips confiding that I'd ruin her with such baking.

"Why don't you get a bit of praise in other subjects too?" said Ronaldson when I told him. "French, for example. It used to be your best subject. Mrs Carew has complained about you twice this week already..."

But I couldn't give a monkey's now about silly little Mrs Carew. Very next day I got a commendation for rapid progress on carrot cake. Undiluted praise was much better than a boring relationship which had not been going anywhere.

And a few weeks later Sal summoned me to a lunchtime meeting in the Culinary Studies suite. None of the peers was called. Was it to be a one-to-one souffle tutorial? But Mr Finch, Head of Business Studies, was perched on a stool in his grey and brown mail-order clothes, prodding a drop scone.

Sal beamed at me, dusted flour from her chest where it always seemed to gather, and outlined her scheme for me to go commercial with my heavy finger food.

"You want me to *sell*, miss? In break?" I settled on a stool.

"Certainly do, Jack. Carrot cake, soda bread, cheesy puffs. The rock cakes, of course. And this morning's drop scones are... mmm, sensational."

"I'll second that," said Finch. "Do you do a sausage roll?"

"But, miss, you may not realise that selling's been banned."

And so it had, ever since kids had arrived in school swollen twice normal size because there were crisp-running profits to be had. Michael and Razza had gone further than anyone else and had managed to make a buck recycling gum. (They chipped it off the bottom of desks and melted it down in Michael's mum's best saucepan with a couple of bags of caster. Then they rolled it on silver foil and cut it peppermint cream style.)

"But this will be an officially sanctioned project," said Sal gleefully. "School inspectors love this stuff and so does the Head."

"Projects with a Business Studies dimension," chimed Finch.

"I see... Where do you want me to do it?"

"Playground, of course!"

"I've retired from the playground, miss." I got to my feet. "It holds nothing for me these days."

"OK. So what about the corridors?"

"Corridors are for fighting and bullying, miss."

"Where else is there, Jack?"

"Library?"

"Crumbs in Mr Schuman's bindings? Forget it."

"So that only leaves one place," I said with a grin, easing back on to the stool. "A place where the project will get a lot of exposure... a place where Lady Disgruntle already sets up every break..."

Sal put a hand on her hip and smiled with dawning awareness.

"Beyond The Dooooor..." I teased.

And they were there.

"The staffroom!" we barked together.

"What about the competition?" asked Finch, suddenly rubbing his beige knee.

"Lady Disgruntle will be swept aside!" cried Sal. "The Head is hot for Culinary Studies right now! It got him a mention in the Times Ed."

"This really should work. Pure competition. And rampant demand. We're gannets at break," said Finch.

Sal handed round the plate.

"To GCSE status for Culinary Studies!" she said, toasting the plan.

"To Business Studies in, er, action," said Finch.

"To the staffroom," I cried and we each whoomphed a drop scone.

On the agreed day Sal came to collect me from Maths before break. We were carrying my tray of wares downstairs when the Head met us.

"Feed 'em up, Jack," he said, chivvying off.

The buzzer had still not gone by the time Sal squeezed my shoulder and I moved Beyond The Door.

There, straight away, was Ms Grundle, all mouth, opening and closing like an old cod as she prepared her tray at the far end of the room.

Hungry teachers shoved through The Door and formed a slavering queue in front of Ms Grundle whose own mouth now simpered moist greetings as she poured the tea.

I was too fascinated by this secret world to feel ignored. I can report that Beyond The Door there is laughter, joking, cussing even; the grumpy ones remain grumpy even there, the whingers whinge and the good ones are good in there too. It is, fundamentally, a human environment.

I had a view of the notice board: Mrs Carew's pretty 'Thank you' notelet to staff ('for the really special CD rack'); Nadir Sharma had had a knock on the head and would probably have 'trouble with even the simplest instructions'; a little poster for a staff stress-busting volleyball game on Friday next to celebrate 'making it this far through the term'. I saw another teacher staring at what I realised was a large bank of form photos. He suddenly yelped with joy having matched a picture to a class list.

"Gotcha! I'll teach you to give me a fake name, you pathetic waste of space."

These photographs, I happened to know, were also for handing to the newspapers when we got murdered.

Meanwhile all the teachers fell on Ms Grundle's stodge and minced it up in their chattering gobs with great gulps of her stewed tea. I didn't notice at first but Finch was trying to open my trading. I sold him a drop scone but he was never going to start a consumer trend. Sal's entrance and noisy enjoyment of my carrot cake, however, did the trick. Those at the back of Ms Grundle's queue came over immediately and the sudden surge of latecomers meant I was soon sold out with about nine quid in my pocket.

The staff herded out with the buzzer, followed soon after by Ms Grundle who ran her trolley over my foot.

"The door," she said, without looking up from her crumby plates and greasy doilies.

"Allow me!"

In the canteen at lunch the dinner ladies had clearly been told to spatter me. I stared one of them in the eye to show I knew whose orders she was obeying.

"It shows how frightened she is already," said Sal when the three of us met later for banking. "How do you think her Ladyship's going to react to these tomorrow?" She pulled a tray of beautiful sausage rolls from an oven.

"But..."

"We'll pass them off as yours," she laughed.

"Excellent," said Finch. "And this is for raising brand awareness..." He presented me with a word-processed sign to hang around my neck.

CURLING'S CAKES
A BUSINESS STUDIES AND CULINARY STUDIES
JOINT VENTURE

"I had it laminated," he added. "Wipeclean – in case the marketplace gets nasty."

Unfortunately Mrs Carew was not quite secure enough in herself to buy from me but almost everyone else did over the next few breaks. Ms Grundle's rage was not the only thing to grow: Finch plotted a sales graph which looked like a cheerful erection, my share of the profit clearing £70. Another mention in the Times Ed and the Head was all over his 'joint venturers'.

Events moved fast. They do in business. Finch made a plan for heavy finger food at the next parents' evening. Sal was expanding the frontiers of canape science and each day my wares grew more exotic: strips of rarebit, the mini-pizzas, angels on horseback negotiating perfect fairy toast jumps. Since she no longer required my cooking skills, I had more time for informal seminars with insatiable mates on life Beyond The Door.

Then, just as suddenly, came Lady Disgruntle's response. She dug out her grease-spattered union membership, made a few urgent calls and was able to dangle the threat of action in front of Bumcheeks who promptly buckled and terminated the project. The thought of her leading her dinner ladies from the canteen to his office was too much.

We wound the business up but, two days later, I literally tripped over the means to our revenge. I saw my old mate Nobbi, the greengrocer, raise his hands just as my foot squished a rotten avocado. I skidded and fell sideways into a pile of fruit boxes, part filled with other dying fruits. Nobbi cackled as he pulled me up out of it.

"Scholars! You want to take your head out the clouds, mate!"

His stall had always struck me as magnificent and at Primary I must have painted more greengrocers than aeroplanes. But now I was staring at it with new fascination, particularly at a plump and weighty fruit I'd never seen before.

"What are these, Nobbi?"

"Canadian cherries – and there's a bastard blackbird sits on the gutter over there and knows just how much they cost. He swoops at 'em..."

"Not the cherries. These."

"Mangoes, Jack. Never seen them before? Jet-fresh, these, from Mother India."

He whipped out a knife, slit it down the middle and rapidly criss-crossed the flesh. The first brilliant cube made me grin. This was up there with caviar. I wanted more, now.

"Go man, go!" Nob removed the flat stone and prepared the other half.

"How much are they?"

"To you, 40p. You wouldn't get a can and a frigging choccy bar from him next door for that, Jack."

I subtracted four tens from my dinner money. He grabbed a handful of cherries and stuffed them in with my mango, swinging the paper bag round and round till it had mouse ears.

"Prefer you to have them than that bleeder." He stuffed the treasures deep into my bag and we stared at the beady bird who got embarrassed and crossed to a distant satellite dish.

My love affair with fresh produce had begun and I quickly established myself as the first and most significant fruit-and-vegetarian in the history of Chevy Oak School.

By the end of the week I had an arrangement with Nobbi. I helped him set up for an hour each morning in exchange for as much produce as I could carry. It beat the paper round and provisioned me for a day of steady consumption at school.

"What's that you got there, Jack?"

At first they took the piss.

"Apple of course."

"A apple? What for?" They'd proudly show their tongues cradling sweets and yank their digits to spurt their cans. But long after they'd finished the day's quota, when their gum too was unbearably tasteless, there was I still eating! With their pretty chocolate bars a sticky memory, the fizzy drinks an ugly fur on their tongues, I simply plucked out another brown bag. Radishes, Antiguan tangerines, Frisbee mushrooms and Congolese bananas. I wasn't darkening Ms Grundle's canteen doors – and I felt great.

From that day on fruit and veg was in. Eating in class, the oldest crime in the world, was never more popular. The dangers of juice on the books and being caught slurping were easily outweighed by not feeling ill all of the time. And most pieces left you with something to hurl at someone, something with very attractive spatter qualities. Eat healthy, chuck healthy. Top stools too.

For Nobbi, whose shop was positioned between the big estate and the school gates, these were the best moments of his professional life.

"It wasn't just the money," he's told me since (in fact he's always waylaying me with memories of that time when he did more business before 8.40am than the rest of the day). "Nah, it was more 'n that, it was the feeling I was contributin' to your wider education."

We used to stand around the stall with our school bags open as Nobbi, like the conductor of a multi-coloured orchestra, handled our orders.

"Greengages, lads! Who wants greengages this morning?"

"Wot are they, Nob?"

"Here mate, try one!"

"Over here, Nobbi, I'll have a few."

A rapid fire into a bag.

"And me then!"

With greengages still in the air he'd be offering outrageous deals on walnuts, dates and celery. Half a cucumber here, a Honeydew there and a citrus symphony everywhere. Then we'd file past his till with our bags open and pay whatever he asked, often accepting an avalanche of cherries with our change. Only Michael ever tried to nick anything: a huge tomato. We cheerfully grassed him up and held him down on the pavement as Nobbi impaled it on that pointy little nose.

Then one afternoon the situation moved on, up a gear, accelerated – always my favourite moment in any campaign. A zitty Year Eleven was being taunted for his dietary habits and Razza had just thwacked him in the neck with an oozing pig of ugli fruit when Ms Grundle tapped me on the shoulder.

"I want a word with you, young man."

"Oh?"

"And the rest of you needn't hang around."

But they needed to all right. Even teachers have to

ask a *bit* nicely in the playground – and this one wasn't a teacher. And she wasn't asking nicely at all.

"Have you had your lunch?"

"Yup," I said.

"But not from the canteen?"

"Nope."

"Why not? You haven't been in all week."

"Didn't know you cared, your Ladyship."

"I don't, at least not about you, Jack Curling. But none of these others have been in either..." She gestured offensively at my back-up.

"Nah!" they cried, pulling beetroot, carrots, all sorts from their jackets. "'Sno need!"

Razza nibbled at a bunch of rocket and the others chewed more noisily.

"This is getting ridiculous. Food is going to waste and that..."

"Means a hole in your lunch profits," I cheeked. "Another one, after all that breaktime business."

"It's... It's impossible to cater for such... monkeys."

"We don't have to take that!" said someone.

"We don't have to take nothing from her," said another.

Ms Grundle stood back, but only to broaden her assault.

"It's not as if any of you is bringing proper packed

lunches. And I know most of you are registered for free school meals. You've got to eat them!"

"She's lary, she is."

"Well outa order."

"I'm not here to debate the matter. I suggest you return to the canteen next week or else I am going to the Head about this."

"And back to your union," I hissed as she turned on her heel to loud jeering.

"Run to Bumcheeks!" we shouted.

"Having a go at what we eat is a sort of child abuse, that is."

"Wait a minute," I said. "The old fart's trying to pull us in on Monday..."

"Yeah?"

"So, listen..." Rhubarb, rhubarb, spanking fresh rhubarb.

I warned Nobbi to expect a larger crowd and he filled his cool room with extra stock. Our publicity over the weekend ensured a huge showing at the stall on Monday morning. And picketing of the canteen that day meant that by Tuesday morning Nobbi was swamped. Most of Years Seven, Eight and Nine took some gear off him on their way in.

"It was magical," he still tells me. "Like a religious

experience. I've never lit a candle to that Saraswati before but now I can't give enough respect to the Goddess of Education."

By Wednesday morning I sensed the movement was peaking. There must have been three or four hundred kids in front of his shop. I stepped up to help Nobbi, soon calling for Michael and Razza to join us. The punters were buying everything: shallots, cooking apples, radishes. We were throwing tangerines ten yards into grateful bags and a volley of toms to another area of the crowd. The bleeding blackbird was busily intercepting cherries. Nobbi just laughed. He was having the time of his life and didn't seem to mind that the bleeding blackbird was going swoop crazy as well.

After morning lessons, classrooms and corridors bore a hint of citrus and then as we poured into the playground even the lingering stench of airline fuel was briefly rolled back. A patch of Heathrow was actually smelling once again like London's own market garden.

But it was eye, not mere snout, which was delighted when I hauled myself up on to the window ledge to peer through the grimy windows of the canteen. It was one of my top moments, a key strand of my establishment and, I think, a mark of my generosity of spirit that I turned back to the mob and singled out one of my less balanced marshals to come and share that great view.

"Michael man! Get here!"

Up he came and together we enjoyed peak lunchtime viewing of the canteen: all the dinner ladies were poised, ladles drawn over steaming troughs – and giggling because there was nothing doing! The place was empty but for Lady Disgruntle, her face school burger-grey. The only other client in the entire canteen was Eugene the Russian from our tutor group, who had, as usual, not a clue what was going on.

"What can you see?" came the cry from our loud boys.

"Wonderful things," I replied. Ms Grundle, suddenly catching the exchange, looked straight up at me through the window. I cocked my head on one side and gave her a big pumpkin smile.

"I had hoped not to have to take you aside ever again," Bumcheeks spluttered that very afternoon. "But sit down."

"Thank you sir."

"Jack Curling, you keep attracting my attention."

"Good, sir. I've been trying to do well, sir."

"You have undoubtedly been trying. But I must ask you one question."

"Sir?"

"What exactly are you *trying* at? You seem to have your own agenda. Is the National Curriculum not to your liking? And the national game? You are never to be seen kicking a ball around like a normal aubergine. And now I am led to believe by Ms Grundle that you have turned the whole school against her burger and chips, what might be described as the national dish... So perhaps you would like to tell me, Jack, in answer to my original question, what exactly are you trying *at*?"

I had no answer for him.

"Mr Ronaldson tells me you're not an aggressive child. Not a bully, at least not of your peers. You are not a 'stiff' – I am aware of the term – yet you are intelligent... in an erratic way. In fact you have much going for you. But you seem to be *going for* different things..."

I had so much else to think about that I lost him. There was Eugene, for example, the quintessential outsider, the only kid in the canteen. What was with him? Could I use my 'erratic' talents to help him? I decided there, in Bumcheeks' office, that I would downsize for what might realistically have to be my last campaign. My two years were nearly up. I would have to meet Dad officially and show him what Chevy Oak was doing for me. A little light social work would be interesting and could round me out as a character as well.

Bumcheeks concluded by requiring me to sign up to some sort of agreement to "show respect to Ms Grundle and her work in the canteen" plus another two-hour invitation. As I walked round a corner, I ran into Sal who enveloped me in a floury hug.

"The icing on your rock cakes, Jack! That was the sweetest revenge."

I thanked her, but I was already moving on – to this new initiative. As campaigns went, however, Save a Russian was to be brief and ultimately over-shadowed by the greatest shock of my life.

Since the summer half-term Ronaldson had grown fed up of entertaining us during morning registration. He'd run out of word games, ancient rock music tapes and quick recipes so he introduced a presentations slot in which the selected pupil had to stand at the front, mumble a few words about any halfway acceptable hobby and hold up stuff as visual aids. We all remembered this as Show-and-Tell from Primary and were duly insulted. Girls, of course, were happy to talk about bands and body-art and clubbing but Ronaldson soon started moaning that no boys were putting themselves forward.

"I'm not going to push *you* into the limelight," he said quietly to me, "but can't you encourage some of the boys, the quieter ones to have a go?"

"How, sir?"

"I don't know, Jack, how do you usually influence people? They're more likely to listen to you than me. Sam, for instance. Doesn't he have some pet?"

"Did, sir. Terrapins. And he's still too upset."

"What about Joel?"

"What about him? I could have a word with Eugene..."

"Eugene? I've hardly spoken a word to him – in nearly two years."

"Nor have I."

But I made sure I caught up with him outside the school gates that very afternoon.

"All right, Eugene?"

He looked up at me in surprise and then looked through me at the arriving bus. As he dug out his pass and stepped up he uttered two words.

"Go Moscow!" he said. And the doors thumped shut.

The next morning after the register, Eugene suddenly advanced on Ronaldson with a carrier bag clenched in his fist.

"I will Show, Sir," he said, "And, Sir, I will Tell."

Ronaldson caught my eye and backed towards his chair with his hands up saying, "Great, Eugene, great. Go ahead."

Waiting until he had absolute silence, Eugene began in a strong low voice. "I am living in your London some time now... and I keep to myself. We are living quiet. I was not unhappy here." He pulled a small bottle from his bag and two glasses to pour a couple of shots, one of which he shoved at Ronaldson. "I do not know you, sir, but still I have liked you. Please, you will drink with me!"

Ronaldson raised his glass.

"So you're off on holiday, Eugene?" he said.

"Friday leave London..."

"For where?"

"Friday leave London – for good or for bad. Go Moscow! Drink!"

They drank and then Ronaldson was hugged by the little Russian. We saw to it that Eugene had a great last day. We toasted his departure with the vodka in the furthest corner of the playground from where we were even able to see some of the Aeroflot fleet, and Razza tried to do a dance which he said he'd seen in a film.

"Back to Russian food, eh?" I said.

"Caviar, caviar, caviar."

"Not really? My Dad likes..."

"Yes, in fact, really really. I eat regularly."

"You like?" I was catching his accent already – and now the scent of a plan.

"Very, very much, I like."

"Where do you get?"

"My Dad. He can get caviar anywhere, even Hounslow. Especially Hounslow." He nodded towards the airport. "Every day. Caviar, caviar, caviar."

"How much?"

"Loads of caviar."

"No, how much money?"

"Little money!"

"Really?"

"Fifty pounds?"

"A tin? A big tin?"

"A tin. You want to see one, touch it?"

I managed to get him into Nobbi's cool room to do the business later in the week just before he left. He said he liked it in there and two years' pent-up silence thawed into a flow of autobiography and ambition. I needed the vodka to keep my blood moving but my head was swimming by the time I asked whether he'd brought the stash.

"Yes, Jake."

"Jack. C-can I see?"

"I have good news for you my friend."

"W-what?"

"I have gotten much more bigger tin for you."

"Much more bigger price, Euge?"

"Much more littler big."

"Let's talk numbers."

"Seventy-five."

I had my entire catering profits in my pocket. There

seemed a neatness about spending the lot in this particular cause. But I hadn't noticed him carrying a bag.

"Let's see the goods," I said, shifting in my chair to sluice a bit of blood around my chilling bum bone. He rolled out from his pocket on to the table a tin decorated with a faint label of an angry fish swimming through a line of Russian writing. It was no bigger than a tin of tuna.

"This *it*?"

"It."

"'S-snot much, Eugene, 'specially for seventy-five quid."

"It is much. Very good price, let me tell you."

"How about sixty?"

"Fixed price shopping."

"Sixty-five?"

"Please no haggle!"

"Seventy then?"

"Not with Russian friend."

"Don't worry. I'm back at seventy-five. Too cold to haggle. Here you go." I spilled my notes and coins on to the table, keeping £1.11 as my entire summer slush fund.

"Good luck." He refilled the glasses. "Good luck, Jake."

"Jack. Look, I g-gotta go, Eugene man." I stumbled out, pushing an eavesdropping Nobbi in to finish the bottle on my behalf as I ran home to hide the tin and myself under the duvet.

I lived through the rest of term with the sense of a job well done. My two years were up. Not only did I have good news for my globetrotting Dad but I had his very favourite nourishment to mark the moment of our vital meeting.

The final afternoon we herded out of Ronaldson's classroom and rushed around for hours in the playground trying to trip each other up and stamp on gulls greedy for the last few crisp packets of the summer. I was happy to let my emotions riot in the space where it had all begun. I loved Chevy Oak and all who roosted in her and I was secure in the knowledge that if anyone turned nasty, staff or kid, I had the power to boot them out of my tree. This was the security I had established and Dad would have to acknowledge it this very night.

He was never home before eight. The caviar would, I hoped, be a stylish start to the proceedings. Would he do his gibbon pout like he had in the Richmond restaurant? Would Mum have some? It was a lovely touch for me to give Dad a reward for recognising my achievement. And then Tommy, Rosie and I would sit on the stairs listening up for a change – to lovely sex in the bedroom.

Razza finally told us that his dad wanted us out because their family were trying to get to the chalet in Southend that very night. We all parted happily with many holiday plans pledged and I walked home alone. But by the time I got to the resident skip on Rockenden Road I was running again. Just couldn't help it! I remember picking up one of Dad's luggage tags, which was on the path, and letting myself into the house. Tommy ran straight into me and I stumbled over the umbrella stand in surprise.

"What ya—"

"Where've you *been*, Jack? I was coming to look for you..." He seemed to be accusing me.

"At school of course. What's the—"

I pushed past and went through to the kitchen where Mum was sitting at the table with her head bowed, rolling an orange between outstretched hands. Rosie was sobbing on the window seat and, from the state of her, had been at it for some time. Tommy came up behind me.

"What's happened?" I asked. The orange rolled some more. Mum and Rosie looked up. "Will somebody talk to me?"

"Dad..." murmured Tommy.

"Yes, what about him?"

"Dad's left!"

"Left what?" My fingers tightened around the tag in my pocket.

"Left us, left home, Jack," said Mum. I grabbed the orange from her and sank my other set of fingers into that.

"Why?"

"Says he can't be happy here. He's going to try living somewhere else, try to be happy somewhere else..."

"What? Where? Why?"

"Let us know. Says he will let us know."

"Can we see him?" My head flailed.

"Needs to be alone. A complete break is better he says... I suppose I agree." Her face creased up and I put my arms around her. She carried on talking but the words went straight down inside the back of my shirt and the orange, stuck on to my fingers like a reluctant grenade, dripped juice down the back of her leggings.

"But what about..."

"What about what, Jack?"

I felt his decision *had* to be linked to my fabulous years, my golden double. The deal had turned sour because he hadn't been able to take my success. He resented having his offer of private school, powered steering, electric wing mirrors, turned down.

Paintballing! When I thought all along I was tying them closer, I'd really been driving them apart. Mum was holding *me* up now.

"What about what, Jack?" My eyes were buried in her collarbone. In that little hollow I saw the possibility creeping up on me that his decision was nothing to do with me, that it was driven by adult forces I had not spotted, let alone understood. The recent anger which us stairfolk had not bothered to decipher because it had not carried our names and our concerns, may have held the answer. But that answer was now as untraceable as the fumes of his car which, Mum said, had taken him off to the airport, passing the playground in which I had been feeling so stupidly happy.

A plane was beating up the sky off to the right, another smashing it to bits over on the left. Nothing compared to what I'd do to him right now. The least you can do, if you're up there, old man, is to take a look down here. I wrenched the caviar from my pocket and stepped out into the garden.

A CANDIDATE HAS JUST BEEN CAUGHT TEXTING IN THE TOILET. MAY I REMIND YOU THAT ANY CONTACT WITH YOUR MOBILE DURING THE EXAM IS ABSOLUTELY PROHIBITED.

All our phones are stacked in a back room. Bet they're all on vibrate, wriggling their way off the shelves.

Rosie was in place on the stairs when I headed down for breakfast. I almost told her there was no more eavesdropping for any of us now the ceiling had fallen in. She had dimples above her eyes. Her tears have to go upwards when she cries in bed and gather in that little string of salt lakes on her forehead.

Tommy was out already and Mum was downstairs making as much housekeeping noise as she could. The TV was on and she was thwacking a duster across her thigh like a rat's tail before injuring another shelf of ornaments.

"Am I disturbing you, love?"

"No, but—"

She spun the tap full on so it roared into a saucer in the sink and fountained back out to spray the floor. She hugged me again and I was happy to go along with it until I realised I was being dragged into some kind of waltz.

"Get off, Mum! There's nothing to dance about."

She spun me away, shovelling eggs straight into the food processor and moaning something about an omelette for tea. The machine leapt into life, she clung on to it and laughed again, throwing her head back as if it were a big bike coming down the mountain. I feared she was going to start shouting about being free – but instead she stopped quite suddenly to stare out of the window and began crying again.

From then on she only entered the kitchen on a Monday to cook the small chickens that we would individually feed off through each week. They sat one above the other on the fridge shelves, every week for months. For something like fun one time I yanked our respective chickens' legs into the positions we'd always adopted on the stairs.

We went away for two, maybe three, weeks. Mum hired a car and we drove from bed and breakfast to bed and breakfast, the breadth of Southern England. She'd ask at the multiplex for the nearest accommodation. When not isolated from my family in front of a screen, I went for long suburban rambles. We had cousins in Southampton who took us bowling. One day Mum saw an old friend in Reigate and in three other places we each endured an encounter with an unenthusiastic godparent.

Back in Rockenden we found the summer dead, or the dead summer decomposing. The skies were trouser grey and more flight paths than ever seemed to have been creased into the clouds.

It's hot in here. And why do they always draw those crappy curtains? About an acre of pink nylon. It's like looking out through giant knickers.

When the first day of school showed up I just hadn't the appetite. I went to the dirty clothes basket and pulled out yesterday's pants. As I walked in robotically, I felt I was going to an alien place, at an alien pace and entirely against my will. I tried to ignore Nobbi though I had to catch the apple he lobbed at me.

"What price thank you?"

Miserably I whirred on – past the gates in fact – and it was only because some kid in my class grabbed me that I made it in at all.

We were a tiny bit late and, because Ronaldson had decided to start the year with a little punctuality campaign, he asked the pair of us to come back in lunch break. I spoke to no-one all day, blanking Michael even. I spent all the lessons head in hands. Of course I forgot to get myself to the detention so Ronaldson tried to keep me back after school, though I managed to slip out while he was patiently listening to Eugene's replacement describing his previous school. I felt exhausted by that day and resolved to fade out, reduce transmission, take Radio Curling right off air.

Next day, of course, Ronaldson got me.

"Er, Jack...?"

I was skulking off at the end of the morning's registration though God knew I had nowhere to go.

"Shall we try again today?"

"Wot?" Rudely to Ronaldson. Another first.

"Those few minutes you owe me from yesterday..."

"Yeah?"

"Just to let you know they have swollen, Jack, to twenty. After school today. *All right, Jack*?"

"Yeah."

But in the end I couldn't be there. He was going to be furious by Monday – so why put myself through that? I took Monday off (another novelty; in both years so far I had won a Chevy Oak Felicitatory 12" Ruler for Full Attendance). At home I was bored by about 9.10am. Mum had long since gone to work and I was in despair.

I went up to their bedroom and monitored incoming air traffic – except now I hoped his plane would just vanish, disappear from the screen. At the same time I missed him badly and, really, I was at home because I hoped he would come for his things. Of course, I wasn't sure what was 'his' and what 'ours'. I confirmed that on his bedside table still sat the plump and cheerful 747 clock that I had bought him on our way back from Ireland. I taxied her around a bit. But after a nervy take-off I couldn't bring myself to arrange a crash landing and instead I touched her down faultlessly on the smooth runway of the not so-smooth-runaway's half of the bed.

Tuesday and I knew I'd have to go in to face Ronaldson. But where did that 'have to' come from? Where would that 'have to' go if I just blanked it? I decided to take a second day off. I wasn't even waiting for Dad any more. He was no excuse for anything. Ronaldson's friendly enquiry on the answerphone was the only voice I heard all day until the return of the remains of the family late afternoon.

By day three Mum was on my case, so I went in. Some girl was doing a presentation on her collection of spent bank cards. She stood on her chair and flicked open a plastic wallet which opened out all the way to the floor, full of them. As the others noisily clapped I shuffled up to Ronaldson and told him a bare-arsed lie about diarrhoea.

"I've just got go, sir..."

He stared at me, disappointed but so bloody understanding. He even opened the door for me but not before Michael had craned under my desk and shouted evilly, "Jack's needin', he really is!"

I scuttled along the corridors I'd loved to strut and then had to hover around Ms Grundle's bins with the truant trash who had, like me, clocked registration and were about to check out for the day. My descent had been rapid but the thought of piling out through the fence with these guys really did loosen my bowels and I hung around after their departure. Then Razza's dad, George, spotted me behind the milk float.

"What's up, Jack?"

"I've got to go, George."

"Ill, is it?"

"Kind of."

"Better go sick room," he grinned.

"Er..."

"Not that kind of ill, Jack?"

"Well..."

"Come on then, if it's the old *homesickness* you're suffering, jump up on board. Micky the Milk here'll be up your road in a minute, innit?"

The milkman grunted consent and I hopped up as he clicked the float to go. George strolled alongside straightening the crates around me and offering some academic advice.

"Nah, you don't want to bother with this year, mate. Effin' waste of time. It's a fill-in year. You won't catch my Razza doing much."

"Cheers, George."

"Way I see it, one less kid, especially you, Jack, the less trouble I have. So you enjoy the ride and don't come back a moment before you feel like it..."

And I was out of there, drumming my fingers on the kitchen table before Michael would have fired the day's first spitball.

·····🐷

Ronaldson rang Mum at work and got the whole story. I bet one of those notices went up in the staffroom: 'Abdul Chowdury is suffering from alopecia. Please do not tell him to remove his baseball cap.' 'Joe Mitchell's grandmother died last week. He may be tearful.' 'Jack Curling is having difficulties at home...'

The next day Ronaldson gripped my shoulder. It felt like he was going to squeeze till tears came out. I filled but didn't spill. I tried to milk the broken home bit but Tommy rushing around like a perfect little button, charming all the teachers with his determination to overcome the domestic deck, didn't help my cause. He'd started at Chevy Oak this term and was still thrilled about the big school stuff, the swearing and the protective goggles in chemistry. He loves football too.

"I'm really trying to get a lot out of lessons, Mum," he purred one evening.

"Good, sweetheart, I'm sure you are. And what about you, Jack?"

Silence.

"Mum, Jack's, er, trying to get out of lessons a lot..."

Tommy was right. I was haunting the school corridors. My bladder, bowels, head – any excuse and

I would wander. I had lost my school bag (I was dangling it over the side of Rockenden's skip when it sort of slipped) so had nothing to put my books in and I'd become confused anyway as to what to bring. At first I folded my exercise books in half, lengthways, and jammed them into all available pockets but soon I was using bits of paper. Then this became an even more practical single sheet, folded into eight boxes, one for each subject. I didn't need much writing space because I only had the energy to carry one hollow Parker and the inner tube of a Bic, as bent as a scorpion, which only ever let ink out inside my pocket.

"Why aren't you writing, Jack?" teacher'd say.

"You've got my book, sir."

"I have not."

"Must be in my bag, sir."

"And?"

"Bag's lost, sir."

"Well, you'll have to write on paper today won't you."

And in ten minutes:

"Jack, why haven't you started?"

"Pen's run out, sir."

"Well, you'd better run out after it, hadn't you? At least go and buy a new one from the library."

And then I would be off into the wood-shiny freedom of mid-morning corridors, eyeballing the classes through the door windows, larking miserably. But I was not to have the run of the place for much longer. Schuman slipped me a notice intended for the staffroom which he'd found on the photocopier. J. Curling was 'on no account to be let out of class. He can be manipulative. He must be contained through what is a difficult time at home.' Signed, the ever-concerned Ronaldson. So I had to start bunking in earnest. I needed a wider, less caring community and I took the milky way out several days each week. My chauffeur was only too happy to box me in among the other empties.

Delivered to Rockenden I wouldn't go in. Instead I wandered far and wide, down streets booming with airliners, squeaking with the window cleaner's rag upon the oily deposits from the sky and twanging with the tinny blare of the builder's tranny as another roof was shored up. Only once did I attract the attention of the police van doing a truancy sweep. I said I'd been sent home and that, yes officer, this here was my very house. And up the garden path I went, wondering who else they had in the van and, more urgently, who was likely to open this front door. But the enforcers were not so interested and drove away before I had to knock.

Then behind a distant mosque and further obscured by a bleak parade of shops I found a playground with swings and a kiddies' roundabout invisible from the road. The place was popular among truants from a range of schools, though I was pleased to see it was out of Chevy Oak's catchment zone. The floor was soft and bungy like the special toddlers' playground at Primary, sweet relief after the hundreds and thousands of paving stones which had my knees deeply aching.

This area was a haven of self-disgust: silent girls on the roundabout and the silent boys on the swings. Up and down, round and round. Not smoking was not permitted and I quickly learnt to roll a joint with one hand so as not to have to give up my swing – and then to smoke even the last two millimetres without my nose catching fire. I took Michael with me once and I could tell he was impressed. That day there was not even any tobacco going round so we rolled up the scrubby leaves which carried enough airline fuel to give a buzz. They said they would be smoking the blossom in springtime which was nice to look forward to.

But the atmosphere changed over the course of my visits. Suddenly we had to sit on our swings and serenade the girls with tacky genital and mammary insults so that they began to put it out or give it back (in a way I hardly understood) as they lay on the middle of their merry-go-round, slowly rotating. One girl had these long legs which appeared from the mingle and kept pushing off from the ground, spinning the pack of them. To my complete surprise I realised I wanted to smoke those legs down to the hilt.

Eventually she replied to our insults on behalf of the girls with such verbal power and challenge that I ran out of the playground. The others stayed, though, and I saw the boys leave their swings and the girls their roundabout to meet in a mashing of mouths on the soft middle ground of the hopscotch.

When at school I drew spliffs on the desks. It was easier to drowse dopily. Michael enjoyed my new strung-out status because it left him free to emerge as more of a player – and my sad presence was tolerated by most for old times' sake.

"Safe, Jack."

"How's it going, man?"

"Later, Jack. Whenever. Whatever."

The next morning Ronaldson was telling us something about exams when I did a huge, noisy yawn. The class roared approval and Ronaldson snapped.

"Out, Jack. Now!"

He got a colleague to watch the others and marched me down the corridor to the Special Educational Needs room.

"I'm not going in there!" I shouted, as hysterical as any kid we had silently smirked at and shaken our heads over in previous years. "*I'm* not thick!"

Mrs Carew came round the corner. I threw myself on to the floor in front of her.

"Miss, help me! You've gotta help me!"

"Here, let me get the door, Mr Ronaldson."

Two regulars were shepherded out for confidentiality's sake and I had just sat down with the feeling that no-one in human history could have fallen so far so fast and from such a height, when a side door opened.

"My name's Jane," said this woman, sitting down near me. I'd seen her at Nobbi's a few times, another old bird after the Canadian cherries. Ronaldson left us. She sat silently and I tried to stare out of the window, which was hard with her looking at me all the time and with Nob's voice in my ear. "You won't make a sale by staring into space. You have to pull 'em in with a look, a word, a song." All that seemed so cheery, so far away. And now I had nothing to sell.

Still she sat silently. A gull looked in as it flew past towards the bins.

I won: she spoke first. But what use was this sort of victory?

"How do you think you're doing at school, Jack?"

"I'm all right."

"Really?"

"Really."

"*All* right, Jack."

"Some things could be better, you know."

"At school?"

"Yeah and..."

"Jack?"

"At home." My voice was quieter. Kids slewed down the corridor, their shoes slapping. Was Tommy out there? Normal noises came and went like emergency vehicles.

"It must be very difficult for you."

"What must be?"

"The situation. The stuff."

We fell silent on this thought. I didn't mind the silence so much now. It gave all my difficulties time to line up. Trouble was the old tears were rolling into position too. But I thought I could cry if I really had to. She probably wouldn't mind.

"Yes, it's very difficult, Miss—"

"Jane... Call me Jane if you like. Do you want to tell me about some of these difficult things?"

"OK, I will..."

"How long has it been difficult, Jack?" She glanced at her file. She should have known this. She had to rummage. I liked her for that. Less the slick professional, more someone's cheerful mum, or gran, rummaging in her handbag for her purse. "Would you like to taste one first, madam?" I had probably said just that at Nobbi's, hadn't I? And probably slipped her a couple of big ones and a wink.

"J-July..."

"Mm, four months, months of adapting to a very different home. When did you last hear from your dad?"

"We got a postcard – that's Tommy, me and my sister. One postcard. Didn't read it."

"Have you spoken on the phone?"

"No."

"What would you say if you could?" she asked.

"Ask him to come home. I'd tell him we can probably sort it all out. Can try anyway."

"That's a good thing to want to say to him. I'm sure he'd appreciate that, Jack."

Silence.

"What else do you think he'd like to know?"

Silence.

"How we are probably. How Tommy's settling in, stuff like that."

"And your sister. Rosie, isn't it?"

"Her too."

"Wouldn't he like to hear how you're getting on, Jack?" She smiled inquisitively, cocking her head. I looked straight at her, suddenly liking her less. "I think he'd like to know you were the happy Jack of the last two years. I think he'd like to hear about some more of your adventures, perhaps, with some news of how you're getting on with your studies..."

I looked at the floor, kicked up the edge of a splotch of gum. There was a knock on the door. Ronaldson ushered my mother in. She must have come from work.

"Thank you, Mr Ronaldson." She turned to Jane.

"Hello..." Always polite. Never gave her teachers the run-around, I bet. "Hello, Jack."

These two changed everything. I was about to call her Jane, nearly did when I said "J-July". But now Ronaldson played the heavy. Jane didn't like it any more than I did. If I had called her Jane, just once, I might have thrown myself at her, hugged her knees, asked her to take me home.

"We are going to be keeping a very close watch on Jack from now on," Ronaldson was saying.

"Good," she said. "It seems he needs it."

"We understand he is extremely upset at the moment but this is not the sort of school which can ignore repeated truancy or condone uncooperative behaviour in the classroom. More to the point, we can't go on applauding Jack's potential. He's got to start converting it into something worthwhile. His achievements in the first two years were not, shall we say, purely academic."

"Oh yes, I mean, no." I could tell she was still mulling over the concept of 'repeated truancy'.

"Well, we think the time has come for him to show what he can do. What do *you* say, Jack?"

I coughed convulsively for a few seconds. But this satisfied no-one and they were still waiting when I came out of it.

"Well, Jack?"

I sniffed convulsively.

"Jack?"

"Yes, Mum." I looked from floor to ceiling convulsively.

"Well, are you going to try? You know, Mr Ronaldson, Mrs – I'm sorry I don't know who you are..."

"Jane Clark. I'm an educational social worker."

Mum's eyes rounded. "An educational *what*?"

"Social worker, Mrs Curling."

"I am at a bit of a loss here. I had absolutely no idea, I mean, I knew he'd been a little low, which is unusual but I thought it was all to do with, you know, happenings at home. But social workers! I really didn't know it had come to that." She almost asked what the neighbours were going to think. She looked from Mrs Clark's eyes to Mrs Clark's feet. She didn't know the extent of the problem, but Ronaldson quickly obliged with details. I knew that letters from school, distinctively franked, had certainly made it, stacks of them, through our door but the last few yards to the breakfast table had seen them go astray.

"Anything practical that can be done, Mr Ronaldson. You have my full support. Now that I *know*. That's a start, isn't it, Jack?"

Ronaldson seemed to be siding with her. He knew what I could do with wool and eyes.

"We will put Jack on full school report from tomorrow which means he must get every teacher, after every lesson, to make a written comment on his performance and I will want to talk to him – in detail – about each day after school. He must also show me that he has all his books and equipment..."

And so it went on. Jane had to leave before Ronaldson was up. She seemed as unhappy as I was at Ronaldson running round and round me with his ball of red tape and his chains.

"Good luck, Jack. I'm sure we'll meet again, either here or at the shop, eh?"

As she left I felt my little coracle was reaching the lip of a waterfall and no-one would be coming over with me – or waiting at the bottom.

We walked home. Mum squawked at me. "Embarrassing" and "embarrassed" were the two key words. I've never seen her so angry. Luckily Nobbi must have been in the cool room otherwise he'd only have gone and said something cheerful as we passed and got himself cored too.

"I'm fed up with you, Jack," she reminded me as her key invaded the lock. "I mean, truancy, now, of all things. I can't understand... I know we've got to talk but I can't face it right now."

"Fine," I said, turning in the hall.

"Don't think about going anywhere. You're grounded until further notice."

Mum sat down. As I left the kitchen I saw her hand reach for the phone so, slave to habit, I settled into my position on the stairs, legs diagonal, feet pointed into a knife and ready, if I heard anything really offensive, to flash down in self-defence.

As I listened my eyes crept up from the bottom of the hand rail along the wallpaper pattern and up to the mirror. My glance shot through the imaginary sibling heads (it had been weeks of nothing for them to listen to) and into the still sunny bathroom where, in a sliver of the mirrored cabinet above the sink, I saw most of Dad's face.

I scrambled up, rushed in. He was splashing water into his eyes as if he couldn't believe them either. All my plans for this encounter – thumbscrews, nutcrackers – came to nothing. I felt blown towards him by the force of Mum's anger and I hugged him, hugged him, hugged him till I could feel his flannel dripping down my neck.

"Hello, Jack."

"I'm so glad you're back... I mean I'm so happy to see you. Hello."

He stepped back and dried his eyes.

"Give me a few moments with Mum, eh, and then come down."

I waited in the bathroom. The greatest eavesdrop of all time and I sat on the toilet out of range with the door closed. But there was no explosion. Nothing as I descended and opened the kitchen door. Mum was by the table and he was at the other end of the room surrounded by possessions he must have collected earlier. I just had time to notice the 747 alarm clock when he said, "I gather things haven't been going too well lately, Jack."

"He's a disaster area, Martin. I wonder why."

"That school—"

"Don't start on *that school*. *That school* has been brilliant. But it has just been the scene of the most humiliating meeting of my life. If you'd been in the area an hour ago you could have come along and turned pink with me. Jack has been playing games with us all – but fooling no-one more than me. He's been playing games, Martin. I wonder why."

"What games, Jack?"

I sat there at the table fiddling with my crisp new report card.

"Come on," he coaxed.

"I don't want to tell you."

"He's been truanting, faking illness, doing nothing in lessons."

"How long's this been going on?"

"Since the end of last term funnily enough. Of course he couldn't officially truant in the summer holidays but, for some unknown reason, we were all of us out to lunch for most of that time. Jack, though, seems to be carrying it into the new academic year."

"My God, Jack, what do you think you're doing?"

"What do you think *you* are doing?" I snapped and gestured past him at his pathetic pile. "And you could leave us one of those speakers."

"We're talking about *you* here, Jack. I know you must have lots of questions for me and there will be time for them all but 'what do you think you're doing' is not one for now. Besides I asked you first."

"God, Martin."

"Well I'm not getting much out of *you*, am I?"

"Fuck you."

Exactly, Mum.

"The mother who is too busy to notice six weeks of dysfunctional behaviour in her son!"

"Sixteen years with you may have affected my sensitivity."

I wanted them to chuck things. Flying plates would have been more eloquent.

"This is ridiculous, Polly. Look will you come and sit down? Jack, please get me some water." I glanced at

Mum. It was surprisingly good management from Dad and solved the immediate future. We were both grateful for something to do though my activity took ten seconds and hers five. Then we were back to square one.

"The way I see it, Chevy Oak has finally and absolutely failed."

"Oh Martin! Can't you—"

"Can I just speak? It may not have failed in its 'duty of care' to our son, it may be now cranking up some catch-all system, some social work as the government obliges it to do, but the fact is, Jack has given up there and we need to be brave enough to face the fact that your dangerous – er, experiment has failed."

"Just watch it..."

"I am living in West London."

"Oh really. Fascinating."

"I'll give you my numbers and you know you can always reach me at work."

"Hello, operator, get me Kuala Lumpur!"

"Oh yeah. Thanks for the postcard, Dad."

"Yes, I have been travelling."

"So've we, Martin. To buggery and back. Sorry we didn't get anything in the post to you."

"Polly, can I go on? A colleague's son messed up his A levels and then went to a tutorial college, a good one..."

"What you call a 'crammer'?"

"He got the results. And this place caters for all needs. I've done some research. Jack's got some government exams coming up, right?"

"Yes."

"They do them at this place. Tiny classes, some one-to-one. A new start. What do you say?"

"I say it's the fucking biscuit, Martin! It really takes the—"

"Jack, what do *you* say?"

Nothing.

"This is incredible. If you think you can come back here and put your son in a carrier bag with the rest of your rubbish, you are a bigger idiot now than the one I married. Did your travels blind you to all his excitement, his happiness, his *achievements* in the first two years? Do you remember, Martin Curling, or was your head always shut inside your lap-top? Honestly, I do believe there's more going on in an overhead locker..."

"I could see he was having a good time, Polly. But was he learning anything? If he had developed any serious approach he wouldn't be so ready to chuck it all in now."

"Don't blame him! How dare you blame first me and now Jack. How dare you!"

Dad looked so desperate and Mum now so hard. I shot out an arm and knocked his water all over the place. This was quite good management too. Mum burst into tears and ran upstairs. Dad went out into the garden and hunched up on the bench in the rain. I couldn't comfort them both, nor did I feel like trying. Beyond the spilt water lay my report card. I stuck a finger on it and dragged it towards the water. It absorbed well. My name, in Ronaldson's writing, smudged and dissolved. By the time I'd got through the pond there was such drag that the corner I was pressing on broke off, a soggy snap.

If someone offers an exit, a way out, it's pretty difficult to continue on the hard road. Anyone can see you should do the difficult thing but I, at any rate, still fancied the exit. If I'd got her name out, Jane might have stopped me. The only other person was Ronaldson and I knew from today that he wasn't going to be any help.

On the other hand Dad had so blatantly broken his side of the bargain by absolutely failing to acknowledge just how brilliantly, creatively, spunkily I had established myself. Part of me *still* thought he'd done his bit of the family-wrecking just to spoil my time at 'that school'. Did he deserve to 'have his go' with my education, especially since a crammer in London didn't sound like posh school with the pavilions and dormitories he used to rave about? Where's the paintballing in that?

I took comfort and some strength from the fact I was now in the middle of the kitchen, no longer skulking on the stairs. If I could divorce the two options from the two weeping brokers, if I could understand it was my education not their education – or their schooling – of me and above all, if I considered what Chevy Oak had become, what it would go on being for me tomorrow and tomorrow, on and on, then why not avoid all the painful encounters, the bemused, increasingly amused meetings with my one-time admirers? Why not leave the Nobbis and the Ronaldsons and the Michaels behind? Why not follow the flight path over to West London?

I heard Dad fumble with the back-door latch as he has always done. There was nothing to say I had to be nice to him in London. In fact I could continue punishing him best by going to London. I heard hints of Mum's quiet descent in the wall by the stairs. Could she perhaps do with a rest from me?

But it was the front door which opened first, Tommy and Rosie rushing in through to the kitchen. They skidded to a halt on Dad's tired smile.

"Hello you two," he said. Rosie went to take Mum's hand and held it in front of her face.

"Hello, Daddy."

"I'm in Mum! I just heard," said Tommy.

"In what?" said Dad.

"Borough football squad, Martin."

"I'm so proud, Tommy," said Dad.

"First round of the cup is Saturday." His voice faltered and he turned away, noticing Dad's belongings by the TV. "The telly's not his, is it?" he said in a panic. "Mum?"

Dad hurriedly started picking up his things.

"Jack, can you give me a hand?"

I followed with a couple of suits which I hung against the left back-seat window as he always does.

"I'm sorry, Jack."

"Yeah, I'm sorry, Dad."

"I'll be in touch. This week."

I didn't want anyone to know my plans at the moment, partly because I liked keeping a secret from this increasingly loud and bullying world and also because this way my plans could easily change. Everything else had changed beyond recognition so why should anyone – he of all bloody people – rely on my plans?

"Cheers, Dad."

He drove slowly away down the street and had me running after him until he waved into his mirror and tipped me a double wink on the hazards.

I was dressed when Mum came in next morning. I'd ironed my trousers till they shone, my tie was a perfect knot and I had chipped off whatever had been on my lapel. My pants were clean.

"Give your hair a brush and you'll be as good as old."

"Good as gold, Mum. I'm going to get all As on report today."

"Where *is* that card? Have you got it?"

"Oh yes, of course. In here." I flashed my inside pocket which glinted with pen clips. I was helping Tommy with his tie in the kitchen when the phone rang.

"Hello, Mr Ronaldson," said Mum. "No it's all right, we're up and about. Have been for quite some time... oh yes, raring to go. He looks quite different. Yesterday was a watershed for our Jack, one way and another. You want a word with him?... Of course. Jack!"

I took the receiver. "Hello, sir. Yes, that's right, sir. Play it one day at a time. Thank you, sir, see you in fifteen minutes. Bye."

Mum stood on the doorstep in her dressing gown and waved us off.

"We're going to make this work, aren't we Jack?" she called.

"Yup, Mum."

"You'll be all right, Jack," Tommy said and grazed my hand with his. We walked in silence until halfway down Rockenden when I did the great big gasp I'd practised in front of the mirror.

"Oh my God," I said. "I've forgotten my calculator. The teacher'll go mad. You go on, Tommy."

But he said he could see it in my pocket.

"I mean my, er, French dictionary. The other teacher'll go mad. I'll catch you later."

He ran off gratefully to catch up a friend. I ducked behind a skip and tore off my uniform like Clark Kent, to reveal my escape jeans and smart orange shirt underneath. I lobbed the bag in after my uniform. Unlike CK I hopped on a bus to Hatton Cross and took the tube into town.

If I were travelling in, say, Guatemala or Austria and a Guatemalan or an Austrian were to ask me where I lived, I'd answer London. Everyone has heard of London. Mind you, everyone has heard of Heathrow, but London has more authority. What's Heathrow got? An airport authority. It's just a gateway and I was through with it.

But although I was definitely a Londoner, I definitely didn't know London. My only point of reference was that exhibition centre. We'd gone there with Grandad years before and I remembered it was in Earl's Court, West London. I thought Dad was probably in the area and I was pleased to see its station marked on the Piccadilly Line map about three feet to the right of Hatton Cross.

I followed the signs from the station and was soon fairly satisfied I was staring up at the façade of the exhibition building. I remembered how much more excited we had all been than Grandad, although it was his trip.

I had learnt Dad's number by heart but my mobile was out of credit. I went into a phone box where I was rattled by the décor. I kept misdialling, and I don't mean to any of the misses and misters on offer. Distracting to find so many arses thrusting into such a confined space, not to say breasts. Eventually though I got through.

"He's not at his desk right now." A quick, male American voice.

"Where is he, please?"

"In a meeting. Who's calling?"

"Jack, I'm his son."

"Jack, why don't you call back in ten minutes?"

"Could you tell me—"

But he'd gone, too busy to tell me the time. Not that, without a watch, I would know when ten minutes were up unless I counted off 600 buttocks or breasts which is just what I set about doing until Dad's voice pulled my eyes down to the cement floor.

"Hello."

"Hello, Jack. It's... good to hear you." His pleasure seemed to fill the box and was suddenly comforting.

"Good to hear you too, Dad."

"Can you hang on just a minute?"

"I haven't got much mon—"

But *he* was gone too. For more than 60 buttocks I heard him pattering around on his keyboard and talking to someone else.

"Look, Jack, can I call you back? Where are you?"

"In a phone box."

"Where?"

"London, of course!"

"Why aren't you at school? I thought—"

"I want to try a new one... your grammar crammer idea or whatever."

"Jack, I'm coming to get you. Where are you *exactly*?"

"I'm outside the Earl's Court Exhibition Centre."

"The Ideal Home! Which entrance – the one..."

"The one we came to with Grandad."

"Just *stay there*. This is great news! If I can get away... yes, I'll be with you – soon."

But I'd been reduced to counting gussets by the time a taxi pulled up with Dad inside. He was hassled. I was hassled. He had had to reschedule a meeting, delay a report. I'd spent the afternoon in a porny phone box. It wasn't a great taxi reunion. He said he would have to take me straight back to his office (which turned out to be more like East London) but he had already arranged for us to see Fortuna College at six o'clock that same evening. Then he would drive me back "to Mum's house".

I had to sit in reception for ages before he came to get me. We got into the car and flogged back West. I thought I saw my exhibition centre again but Dad said it wasn't and eventually he parked in dog's turd with the Victoria & Albert Museum, he said, just visible. I've since discovered it was the Natural History.

The frontage of this Fortuna College seemed a little cramped but I was sure it ran deep. Some lush girls were sitting on the front steps. Dad explained ourselves to the secretary which eventually flushed out a fat man from behind a big door.

"Welcome," said Mr Mortlake.

Inside his office he sat with his palms up as if expecting Dad to lay our dilemma, suitably dolled up and powdered, upon them. Which he did, adding that a colleague had said Fortuna was the top crammer.

"Very kind, very kind," said Mortlake. "Though I have a problem with that c-word. It does so bring to mind pate de foie gras." He moistened his lips. "Don't you think, Mr Curling?"

"I'm more a caviar man actually," quipped Dad.

"We have a more holistic approach to education at Fortuna. An all-round baking, if you like, Aga-style, but necessarily delivered with the speed and intensity of the microwave."

"And this will prepare him in the main subjects for these government exams?"

"Oh yes, of course, the suddenly sacred SATs exams. I understand the urgency of the situation and we can certainly deploy appropriate teachers, from tomorrow if you so wish. He may feel a little... isolated at first. Most of our students join us later, especially after A level." He gave a little clap at the beauty of a business which dealt in failure. "However there is no reason why we can't achieve great things with Jack and send him on his way as contented – as well-cooked, yes! – as hundreds of others." He stood. "You will need some time to mull it over. Can I have you shown round?"

Afterwards we picked our way through snog-knots of students out on to the pavement and into a busy café which was even more knotted.

"Well, Jack? What do you say?"

"Why did you have to mention caviar?"

"*What*? Did I? Caviar?"

"Course you did. When he—"

"Keep your voice down."

"Why?"

"Because people are looking at you..." And they were, a group of student types of all ages in a booth, looking and smirking. "Of all the questions anyway! What's caviar got to do—"

"You really didn't remember, did you? And you still don't!"

"Look, Jack, can we just discuss this college now? I'd like to get it sorted out this evening and you have presumably come up to London because you are interested."

"Presumably."

"Well, put it this way, Jack – are you going back to Chevy Oak tomorrow or are you going to go on wandering the streets like a delinquent?"

I sat in silence, drinking in these bitter options with my ginger beer. Then I got suddenly to my feet and said, "Have me crammed then."

After Mortlake had stopped whinnying with pleasure about our speedy decision-making, enrolling took about half an hour and a load of Dad's cash. It was all just about sorted with Mum that evening. She was tired enough of me to agree with Dad that I should try living in West London with him.

MAY I REMIND YOU THAT YOU HAVE TO BE ACCOMPANIED TO THE TOILET BY A MEMBER OF STAFF. DUE TO THE RIDICULOUSLY LARGE NUMBER OF REQUESTS YOU MAY HAVE TO WAIT A WHILE BEFORE YOU CAN GO.

Wok, ironing-board and television were just about all Dad had in his flat – plus a sofa-bed which was still polythened inside when I got it open.

He woke me up at six the next morning.

"What's happening?"

"Work, Jack, the world of..."

"What?"

"I have to be at my desk by seven."

"Have you *always* worked so hard?"

"These last few years, yes. We haven't had too many breakfasts together, have we Jack?"

He had turned his attention to heavily-packaged croissants which he stabbed at with a huge knife. He had bought me every sort of cereal and spread. Dad kept breaking off from eating to check his briefcase and fiddle with his tie knot, though it seemed fine. He looked at me in the mirror.

"Now, Jack, I've done this map to the college. Are you sure you don't want us to talk it through together?"

"Dad! I can manage. Are *you* all right?"

Sweating on an October morning, he adjusted his tie again.

"Fine, I've just got a lot on today, this week, in fact, before my next trip. I must go."

I followed him to say goodbye. He kept looking behind him as if worried I wouldn't make it to the door.

"Good luck, Jack. It's all going to be all right."

"See you this evening. *Darling...*"

"You've got your key and my number?"

"*Yes, Dad, I have.*" I had just got back into bed when I heard the lock give. He came running into the room brandishing a watch in a box. "I forgot this. I bought it for you in Vancouver. You will use it, won't you?"

·····

I reached college despite a more interesting morning journey than I usually enjoyed. In place of the grassy roundabout at the bottom of Rockenden there was Hyde Park. Instead of Nobbi's I had a cybercafé, an auction house and an umbrella store. For a couple of biddies in house coats and a stream of Chevy Oak kids I could stare at anyone from bag-ladies steaming with morning dew to the cool young clicking self-consciously to work. The noise of London was different too: it was wraparound sound whereas Heathrow's noise drops on you from above. I'd been dropped on long enough. London sounded much, much better to me.

I had to meet Mortlake at 9.30 to get my 'schedule'. We had decided yesterday that we would concentrate on the three subjects in which the government could not wait to give me a good examining: Maths, Science and English. I wandered up the street a little where two people were kissing, the man leaning the woman against a letter box. A white van honked. By the time I got back Mortlake was telling me I was late for my first lesson and snapping his fingers at me, as at a cheeky roadrunner who didn't want to hop into his oven. I skittered up the stairs, sick at the thought of messing up my new start at the very beginning, giving the other students a chance to stare. I had trouble with the handle too but when I entered all I saw was a thin man in glasses and a safari shirt sitting alone at the table.

"You must be, Jack Curling." A posh voice but the plums were small and halfway up his nose.

"Am I the only one, sir?"

"You are. You won't need to call me 'sir'." He never did tell me what he wanted me to call him. I don't think he wanted much out of life, least of all to teach me Maths.

Afterwards I had a 'free' which I spent sitting on the Fortuna steps wondering whether I would ever meet another student. I'd had more fun in that phone box. The thought prompted me to check the mobile for messages. One, from Mum.

Next was Science. Again I was alone, this time with a fast-talking woman dressed brightly and wearing mauve lipstick. She rattled through her plans for my Chemistry, her smile as bright and steady as the Bunsen burner which played in front of us. She said she would also be doing me for Physics and Biology and her eyes gleamed at what we might both perform on a Fortuna frog.

At lunchtime I pushed my way into the same café we'd visited yesterday and again it heaved with students speaking loudly and confidently. They all smoked and took coffee only for their lunch, packed tight into the booths, lolling on each other, smoking each other's cigarettes and snogging each other's friends. Perched on a bar stool, teasing out a chicken and sweetcorn sandwich, I had a particular view of the noisiest booth which also seemed to contain the lushest girl. She grabbed my helpless eye, and held it tight. Her breasts reminded me of the beautiful Roman slaves' ones in Asterix and enslaved me now. She was the best booty in a boothful of slick girls and boys with their shades riding forehead. But next to her sat a much younger kid, about my age, who looked utterly bored.

Thanks to my new watch, I was at my desk for English before the teacher arrived. I was expecting a Mr Floyd but not a geezer in a leather jacket with bangles in his ears and wicked sideburns tusking him like a boar.

"Hi, I'm Lionel Floyd," he said, throwing back his chair and slumping down, "And I'm knackered. You must be Jack." He gave me a big grin and stuck out his hand.

"Hello," I said.

"Now all we need is Dan."

The door opened and in he came.

"Jack's just doubled our class size, Dan! We've got company from now on." Dan looked as thrilled about the idea of company as he had been at lunch but he recognised me immediately and nodded a greeting. Lionel flicked his hair back, smoothed a tusk and said he and Dan weren't doing anything they couldn't interrupt so we might as well introduce ourselves more fully.

I can't remember what I said – or what Lionel said – but Dan Jackson-Fain explained that he was from Queen's, New York which he seriously missed. From nowhere came a bolt of purest envy, that he could have seen through London already, the city I was finding quite cool.

"I was at a school in Pimlico but it didn't work so Dad transferred me and, no offence to you guys, I hope he transfers us all right back to New York tomorrow."

We looked at a poem, an interesting one which was also funny in parts and Lionel pointed out one or two things the poet was doing deliberately which Dan and I tried to argue were fluke. We let Lionel outmanoeuvre us in debate during which I looked at my watch a few times. It caught the sun beautifully and, despite the thrill of literary criticism, I naturally thought about trying to blind Dan or illuminate the teacher's groin. Instead I let the reddish speck flit around the walls.

"Russian naval officer," said Lionel, immediately picking up its route. I looked blank. "The reflection of your watch... it is flickering like a Russian naval officer."

I still didn't understand.

"Like a butterfly, a red admiral."

"And that," said Dan, "is likely to be a simile."

"Well caught, Dan. Mr Jackson-Fain's in charge of similes and he's getting quite good at trapping them. We have a vacancy down in metaphors. If you like, Jack, I'll put you in charge there..."

"Don't mind," I replied, though I hoped I'd find them in the same place Dan hunted.

"It's the way he teaches," he told me afterwards as we walked down the stairs from Lionel's sunny room. "You'll get used to it. He irritated me to hell at first but I can't read a simile now without zapping it."

"That's bizarre," I said.

"'Bizarre!' 'Bizarre!' So British! You know, I don't need any more friends. I've got a string of them back home. But a single British one might be acceptable..."

I think I said it was OK either way by me too and dared to hope he might take that as an application. It felt a little dangerous to be so keen. But after weeks of shut-down I wanted to transmit something. Radio Curling was back on air, target audience of one.

He allowed himself to be pulled off the bottom

step and into a hug on the landing by that beautiful slave girl. She gave me a light blue flash of a glance over his shoulder and then buried her face in his hair. I went to Maths, Science and then back to Dad's flat for a boring weekend: park, one trip to cinema, Dad's rubbish choice, Chinese restaurant (ordered offal: my rubbish choice), more park, homework invigilated by Dad, some phonecalls with tearful Mum. I was impatient for something to give. This was a pitiful way to be spending my time.

At Fortuna on Monday the talk was impressive. The weekend's partying had evidently been huge. Eighteenths, twenty-firsts, Hampshire, Sussex. One girl insisted Cornwall had been unparalleled for naughtiness. Others had been so wasted by the Thursday-Friday city scene that they vegged and quiched and chilled in parentless houses around London. From what I overheard, everyone seemed to work considerably harder at their weekends than at their weeks when they were microwaved *à la Fortuna*.

We both had to read out our homework compositions. Dan's portrayal of American life was exotic in both mood and grammar. When the time came I picked my way expertly through my messy sideswipe at a Hounslow existence – reading through the milk splotch, and the butter window – so it sounded fluent enough.

I smiled a bit shyly over my similes as Dan made snaffling motions with his hunting hands and with a sudden grab of my own I pocketed what I thought might be a metaphor as I read. Of course Lionel was delighted, but I was much more strongly aware of Dan's scrutiny. He seemed to be examining the components of my face, in between doodling. Then, as I laid my sheets back on the desk, he started clapping. Lionel joined in.

I escaped from his praise after class to catch Dan on the stairs.

"What have you got now, Jack?"

"It'll be Science or Maths..."

"What a pity." He was suddenly hamming up a plummy English accent. "I have some properties you might be interested in, Mr Curling..."

"What do you mean?"

"Some properties – of the sort you might be looking for."

"I doubt you have any appropriate, young fellow," I replied in my lame American accent. I had no clue what he was on about but, since it seemed to mean more of his company, I decided to bunk. "But I can take a few moments to look over what you've got."

We jumped off the bus at the King's Road and ran through streets of small white houses, as shiny as smeared toothpaste in the afternoon light. Eventually Dan stopped running.

"Obviously, sir, it depends what you are looking for but I have some very interesting residences in this prime tranche of Chelsea."

"I'm attracted to the area," I said, fascinated.

"Then let us take a look at one, shall we?"

He unlocked a front door and led me into a house which had looked normal from the outside but which I now saw had been utterly hollowed. The first floor had vanished, making a fantastic yellow-walled cavern.

"Yes, an unusual line," he cooed. "Unusual owners too. Take a look through here."

We went into a long low room stretching into the garden. A table ran down its length. Floor, walls and ceiling were blood red. A collapsed snaggle of crimson candles lay spent in a huge crystal centrepiece and there was evidence of recent feasting.

"Somewhat carnivorous, the owners are..." He looked at me and I felt the deconstructing eyes. "Well, sir?"

"I'm impressed," I said, unable to maintain the accent. "Do you live here, Dan?"

"Diana Jackson does. She is my mother." I was excited to discover he was from a broken home. We returned to the pavement and walked briskly on, turning left into the next street and left again.

"And this," he said, introducing another key into another toothsome house front, "is where my father lives. In fact, from the noise within, I'd say you are about to meet the Partnership, architects to some of the world's more long-suffering clients."

The Jackson-Fain Partnership was in the kitchen, tall Diana Jackson with variegated-blond hair, thin feet and toes with red nails like a row of exclamation marks and big Doug Fain, black-silver hair and beard. He wore a suede waistcoat and glasses so fragile you only saw them when they caught the light, which they did frequently because his head was always moving.

"You are welcome here at any time," Mrs Jackson told me after the introductions.

"Dan's friends are our friends," said Mr Fain, "especially when they are such rare and special creatures." He roared with laughter and hugged his boy, who smiled patiently out from under an armpit.

"He means over here," said Diana. "Since arriving in London Dan has been unlucky enough to meet only 'jerks'. Now, at last, he's met a Jack! Are you a genuine Londoner?"

"Oh yes, we're on the A to Z," I blurted stupidly. "At least one half of our road is." They looked nonplussed.

"I mean I live near Heathrow." But this must have sounded even more foolish and they laughed. I laughed too because I realised I no longer lived near Heathrow. I explained everything over the strongest coffee I'd ever drunk, Doug's brew. By the time I had filled them in with my full domestic details both Diana and Doug had made separate excuses and left us.

"Do you want to see upstairs?" said Dan.

This house of Doug's was beautiful. Books tracked us throughout the tour, great big art books punctuated by sculptures, paintings and bizarre furniture "banged together by Dad in his spare time," commented Dan, "and already falling apart!" Mirrors everywhere, working the light around the interior and shooting it out again, much improved by the experience. A window overlooking the garden revealed a Japanese-style bridge which took off over what looked like a small, glass spaceship embedded in the grass – and then continued its arch over the back wall. The Partnership, hand in hand, were just now walking over it. "He built the bridge as well. It goes through to that house the other side of the block," Dan explained, "which they use for entertaining. They've probably got a dinner there tonight."

"What's that bubble thing?"

"A Jacuzzi! The first project they have ever worked on together, at the same time, and it is already two months late. They each blame difficult clients!"

I flushed with envy, a sudden image coming into my head of our stairs and the prickly carpet and the fussy patterned wallpaper. I turned from the window. We found his room in the attic eventually and sat talking for the rest of the afternoon. I began to think he might be a little lonely – though in a much neater, cooler way than I was – and when I got up I was sure we were friends.

On the way down I met the rest of his family, which just about finished me off.

"So *you're* Danny's buddy," said the slave girl. She had his eyes and mouth, I saw them now. "What's your name?" Dan's eyes and mouth, slightly longer face, beautiful breasts. Asterix would take an overdose and storm Rome for her.

"Jack," I said.

"Nena, meet Jack," said Dan, behind me. "Jack, my sister Nena. What can I do?" He shrugged because she simply shone. It was a crime not to look at her and if you committed it – if you tried to look away to show her she wasn't everything to you already – she got you back swiftly and punished you with an ensnaring smile.

"Give Jack a drink? He's looking hot," said Nena, about to be phoning someone. "Are you the writer by the way?"

"I must go." I couldn't say more. I could barely breathe.

"See you at school. We must go to the 'pub' or something..." She smiled and carried on talking. I listened briefly before realising, with some confusion, that she was talking into a tiny phone somewhere in her tresses.

Over the next few weeks I spent more and more time at the Jackson-Fains' and was able to irritate Mum by saying that all my real friends lived in Chelsea. I realised how unusual it had been to see Nena at home but on the landings and in the nooks of Fortuna I had gorgeous sightings and the occasional friendly comment – if not exactly pub trysts. Doug and Diana looked after me very well when they had time, but they had a lot of other people to look after very well and a large chunk of gutted stucco to do it in. So Dan and I had the run of the rest including the longest back garden in Chelsea.

At least once a week, sometimes three times, we ate huge portions of their catered dinners with our fingers while the guests chinked crystal at the other side. Doug would often heft back across the bridge in his amazing tux and grab a hairy handful of our rich pickings, taking a break from society. I had coped with their coffee through truckloads of sugar. Now I learned to enjoy Tokaji pudding wine. There always seemed to be an open bottle to freeze down to slush and suck up through straws.

I was used to arriving home after Dad, in the taxi he paid for on account out of what I called the guilt fund. Suited me. I was too high for public transport. My plans for the week I sketched for Dad in messages on his office voice-mail. Pleased I was enjoying the crammer life, he couldn't quite see why and didn't have the time to investigate further. I played him off against Mum who had no idea how much he was now travelling.

But just as the cold wet streets of Chelsea had become so brilliant for me, a Jackson-Fain plan to vacation in the USA came into view. Dan was excited and there were more and more conversations in which I couldn't join. They did ask about my plans but what could I say? Everybody goes to Heathrow at Christmas but only sad Jack stays there.

The last day of term Dan brought me something flat and soft, wrapped in a bit of shiny paper in a roll and a half of tape. I tore into it on a Fortuna landing. It was a dark purple waistcoat with the odd faint orange stripe. I put it on and felt suddenly sexy. Crazy to say but a strip of cloth with two arm holes and a stained lining was turning me on.

"You like? Nena and I went to a real London street market for it."

Suddenly Nena was there.

"Come on, Jack, let's see it. Very literary. Yes! I was right, eh, Dan?"

"She chose it," he said as she ran the back of her fingers down my buttoned-up front.

"Maybe wear it loose." She smirked. The friend who loomed now behind her was too tall and beautiful, too busy working his hair – and hers – to be interested in this intimacy. Not that he was invited. Nena plucked open one, two, three buttons until I clumsily took over the rest, accidentally scratching one of her fingers.

"Happy Christmas, Jack."

"We gotta go," said Dan. "Dad's booked theatre."

"Are you flying to America tomorrow?"

"First thing. See you next year, 'mate'."

"What do you *mean*?"

"January, you mug!"

He suddenly hugged me and beat my back like a carpet till I pushed him away, managing to laugh. I ran all the way to a second-hand bookshop in Earl's Court, bought some posey poems and wrote 'Happy Xmas, Dan, Love Jack' into the front. I walked back and, drawing blood on one of their bloody jolly wreaths, thrust it unhappily through one of their bloody shiny letter boxes.

Next morning, with my adopted family slipping away from me through the stratosphere, I lay in bed turning my mind slowly to my own people and their Christmas plans.

"I've got a few days' golf," Dad had said.

"When did you take that up?" He could still produce the occasional surprise, dull aftershocks from the big one.

"I haven't really. I might not go."

"But you're not coming home?"

"No, Jack. You know that wouldn't work. I can't just pitch up anyway. It's not my home any more."

"I could invite you. It's still mine, you know."

"I think Mum has to do the inviting, don't you? And even if she were to, I'd have to feel like accepting, wouldn't I?"

"Yeah, yeah..." This was all hyper-hypothetical. "What do you want, Dad?"

"What do you mean?" He sounded hunted.

"For Christmas!"

"Oh, I don't know."

"Golf balls?"

"Definitely! Dozens!" We always ended conversations like this, falling away with relief and some brittle laughter. The pesky balls, though, were expensive so I only bought him three.

Mum wanted me home straight away for the annual photo which, in these unsettled times, she'd only just remembered. She was coming up to London with Tommy and they would collect me after they had been shopping. The bumpkins got lost and a bit stressed on their way to the King's Road. I enjoyed showing off my knowledge as we wandered. But all too soon we were home for good old Christmas.

I wore my waistcoat for the photo. Tommy had a new football club strip and Rosie a long T-shirt.

The Queen provided more optimism than the rest of us that Christmas. God save her, I thought, and God help us. Mum's sprouts were grey and, for something to do, I ate far too many.

On Boxing Day I rang Dad at some hotel somewhere.

"Hi. How's things?" he said. "Happy Christmas. I've got presents for you…"

"Don't worry."

"Tell Rosie and Tommy."

"Why don't you?… OK, I will. How's the flog?"

"Eh?"

"The golf."

"Thanks for the balls. They *were* great."

"Who's with you, Dad?"

"A whole gang, some of the younger ones at work, with their partners..."

I drew the conversation to a close before I could feel sorry for him.

When I went back to London I sensed that things would be different at college. Merriness had been replaced by January and my exams approached. Dad, I knew, was coming in to talk to Mortlake, which is more than I'd done since October. And I correctly guessed my teachers would have delivered their assessments to his fragrant office.

But, like all teachers, they were fudging it. If they admit kids don't have a prayer it reflects badly on their own work. They prefer to wait till you plough the exam and then they can blame it on poor revision, exam nerves, overcast conditions, misreading of the question – anything to leave *them* in the clear.

"It all seems to be coming together for you, Jack."

"I haven't begun the real charge, Dad."

"And you've made this good friend. They sound a very – civilised family... Don't worry, I won't pry. I used to hate it when..."

"Dad, I've got to go."

"I just want to say – you get these exams and we'll

have you in a really good school for September. You'll have put it all behind you once and for all." That might have been a tear in his eye. I could only see one eye, one tear, because he was staring out through the windscreen. I gave the hand on the gearstick a quick pat.

"Can you stop, Dad? I'm going to Dan's."

"Fine. Will I see you later? I thought we might catch a mov—"

I was so early in Chelsea I had to loiter, wandering back and forth between their front doors. Dan sent me a message from the airport – SAW UR HOUSE AS WE LANDED. GT OUTA BED & GT BACK 2 LONDON!!! When I got cold I disappeared into a café from which I eventually watched their arrival. I nursed my tea, trying not to be too overwhelmed with relief at their safe return. After twenty minutes I could resist it no longer and hammered on their door. They cheered when they saw me!

At the last minute they'd "blown up to Maine" as well as through New York. I actually thought Dan had grown and didn't recognise him in some of the beautiful black and white photos fanned out on the table. I recognised Nena. She gave me a hard time because for once I was not wearing the waistcoat. I was happy to be given any of her time at all.

Dan had a list of galleries and museums which his folks were insisting he saw while in London. I agreed to go along. He stared at exhibits, grabbing details with his quick eyes: Chinese wine cup in the British Museum for example, the corner of a tapestry with a dachshund toying with a frog. Instinctively he seemed to point out things I liked. It troubled me that my instinct didn't discover these things before he did. Sometimes we had to pretend to be old friends – or total strangers – meeting noisily in the middle of some huge exhibition space. We got sent out of the café at the old Tate for unpacking and laying out a sumptuous picnic, the remains of a Jackson-Fain banquet.

The Jackson-Fain Partnership also pushed him towards key buildings and we ticked them off one by one.

" I had a stiff neck as a kid. It was always, 'Will you just look up there?'"

On the top of a bus coming back from Greenwich (where we had been advised mysteriously to look at the hospital) I told him about stairlife at Rockenden. I wanted to tell him everything about our family and Dad's betrayal.

"Will you just look up there?" he said as we passed St Paul's and pointed to the lantern teeming with tourists. "Let's go!"

We went up at pace and shouted as we peeped down from the windy nipple. He had the Monument on his list so he made me run up the tight little stairs, snapping at my heels and shoving me past tourists until we popped out and peered down again.

We went stair crazy after that, running down tube spirals, our heels slapping on the metalled edgings. We ran down department store steps. We ran down up escalators and up down ones. We ran up and down all the unexpected flights between different bits of central London. We ran faster and faster but nothing blurred. I could write you a list here of every up and every down we made.

But our favourite stairs were the Fortuna's flights which connected Lionel's sunny hutch with Mortlake, who regularly shouted at us for running. Copulation in the corridors, he could tolerate. Narcotics on the landings, fine. But us two running out down into our city he couldn't handle.

One day Dan said he wanted to introduce me to his great aunt. I expected another Chelsea door to be thrown open. I expected drapes and papery hands. I certainly did not expect to have to chase Dan along the lost paths and through the sunny green tunnels of St Pancras & Islington Cemetery.

"Was she Jackson or Fain?" I brushed epitaphs, hoping I would find her before Dan, taking care not to lose him.

"She was so beautiful they made a statue of her as an angel. She must be here somewhere." He dived off in search. I kept my eyes skinned for wings. We were in the very middle where it was quite silent but for Dan skittering through undergrowth. Suddenly a twice life-size statue reared above me. I stepped back to examine the face. The resemblance to both Dan and Nena was astonishing. 'Called Home,' I read. 'Arabella' but the stone had begun to disintegrate. '1872–189...'

It looked like a three. I shouted for Dan who broke through a bush to reach me. "Well found! That's her, dead by twenty-one."

Arabella was standing on top of a stone room with wooden doors.

"We kind of adopted her when we came here first. She's not exactly blood but she likes us to visit. Come on into her mausoleum." He pulled apart the collapsed padlock and pushed open the doors.

I hesitated.

"But, young man, fear not. She likes you..."

As soon as I was inside, he pulled the door shut. The only light now was a thin sun bar from a small grill in each wall. It was enough to pick out Dan's face as he sat on a stone on the far side. I leant against the wall, sitting on the dusty floor.

"No-one in the whole world knows where we are," he said. "Terrible things could be happening and we wouldn't know..."

"Terrible things could happen in here and—"

"No-one would know?"

"No-one."

"Aunty might tell."

We sat on in silence, watching the grates lose their sunlight, darkening to purple grey grids. He kicked my foot and asked me if I was happy.

"Yeah, course."

I had been happy once before. Running around the playground on the last day of term thinking of the caviar summit, for instance. But that was stupid-happy, naïve-happy. Running up and down London, on the other hand, lying on Dan's bedroom floor listening to Nena's music below, here now, was proper happy.

"Yeah, well I'm going to be even happier with this London of yours when the mighty Jackson-Fain Partnership finally opens that Jacuzzi! Ever had one, Jack?"

"Nope."

"Oh, you'll love it!"

Eventually we ran back through the greenery and emerged on to the gravel to the surprised and then suspicious stare of the gatekeeper, who'd have had a few questions to ask of us if we hadn't sprinted off down the steps with his answers.

But I am soon faced by another question. Although the Jacuzzi is ready the very next week, am I ready for it? Certainly I have seen hot tubs before, even spent a few gritty minutes in the one beside the Hounslow swimming baths, and I certainly have my trunks in my bag when I get to Chelsea after a terrible day of Maths and Science.

Dan says everything is ready.

"The architects themselves took the inaugural plunge last night."

"And?"

"Big success! Though they fought over the throne." He explains that the Jacuzzi has one much grander seat, wider and with more jets, surrounded by lesser niches. "Come on, I'll race you for it."

We run through the garden, round the outside of the bubble, and enter through a clever doorway under the bridge. Dan throws the switches and the water starts to boil. The glass, blue-tinted, casts a magical light, enhanced by low wattage studs encircling the bath. We've been in a tomb. Now we are in a womb.

"Wow!"

"Like it? Come on then, Jack. First one in gets the throne!" Dan goes into the changing pod. As I make to follow I realise I have left my bag in the house. I tear off my clothes, climb into the surge and establish myself in the prime position.

Dan comes out in his knee length surf pants and laughs. He has found the music buttons and some more for the water which now boils with further jets. He sits across from me in his humbler accommodation and we both laugh and laugh. This is wonderful.

I feel so strung out. I kick out my legs. I raise my arms and put my hands behind my head. Dan does the same and I see the hair under his arms. I make the monkey face at him. He braces his chest. Do my muscles look like that?

"Your Highness," he mocks, now replacing his estate agent drawl with butler's crawl, "I crave your attention."

[wearily] "Oh how tiresome, is there a flunky in my bath, skulking in the steam? Speak from the mist, mere courtier."

[unctuously] "May I suggest a refreshing spank, your Magnificence?"

[trying to focus through the steam] "Who, pray, am I giving audience unto?"

"Sir Barnaby Thwacksome, your Highness."

"Keeper of the Royal Birch Twigs?"

"At your disposal, Most High and Mighty."

[with mounting and justified indignation] "Tell me, little speck of insignificance, what gives you the right to make such a suggestion?"

"It is not only my right but my duty to spank the Kingly hide after a right royal tub."

"I was not aware I had promoted you to Thwacker of the Royal Butt." [daringly] "Besides, Lady Nena of Chelsea enjoys that privilege..."

"I humbly beseech you, Your Highness..."

"Your snivelling self-promotion is unbecoming, Sir Barnaby. I've a mind to leave you here till your doodle shrivels and your liver inflates..."

"But you won't, will you, your Manliness?"

"Wherefore ever not?"

[triumphantly and terrifyingly] "Because, Most Excellent Omnipotence that ever outshone the majesties of Olympus, you're as bare-arsed as a plucked turkey."

I look down at the churning water around me.

How the hell does he know? Dan smiles across, most pleased with the allegation which I still haven't managed to deny. To make matters worse, I can make out a slim form crossing the overhead bridge.

Soon I follow Dan's eyes up to the door to see Nena, comfy in white towelling robe, camera in hand.

"So you boys are here already to destroy my peace, are you? I must punish you with a bathtime picture."

Dan moves towards me as Nena tries to get an angle on us. Her robe opens and I look at Dan in panic.

"Hey, babe," shouts Dan, reaching an arm round my shoulder, "a picture of Jack in the Jacuzzi!" He looks down and pinches my shoulder. She takes the shot, drops camera on robe and enters the pool. Topless! Hard on me though it is to preserve any calm, I am determined to try. Dan goes over and grabs Nena's waist. She shrieks as he lifts her up, for me I can tell. He knows what he is doing.

She turns on the wave machine and swims against it for a minute or so. The extra undercurrent further engorges me, my desperate life, and in panic I hold out my hands to stop Nena from being thrust on to me.

"Hey, Jack, cut that out!" She is laughing, thinking I am groping her. Dan turns off the waves and, to my new horror, the rest of the jets as well. The whole tub suddenly stills. I cross my hands over my lap. I try to shrink. I just get bigger. I surge across to the button to revive the jets. Dan blocks me but I get there and hit the control. Out of breath and overheating we all settle back. General bubbles.

"Enjoying yourself, Jack?"

Her breasts are sort of staring at me.

"Oh, very much, thank you, Nena."

"Oh *very much, thank you*, eh?"

I ask whether she likes it and how her life is going and – anything to divert attention from me. But I know I am failing.

She pushes back her hair with arms raised to show smooth, just darker-pink pits. "Suddenly I feel sexier in here than I have felt for a long time." She smiles. "Do *you* feel sexier here, Jack?"

Oh dear.

"I feel pretty... sexy... really," I manage.

"I feel pretty... sexy... really," she mimics, her toes now kneading my knee.

"Well, what do you want me to say, Nena?" I am desperate and now sound it. "What do you want?"

"You to loosen up, Jack. You're a good-looking guy

but you're so – I don't know."

"Hard?" This, helpfully, from Dan. "Hard to get to know, I mean..."

"I guess." She closes her eyes and, after two minutes of the three of us silently soaking, she says, "I gotta go, boys," and stands up.

I loosen up my eyes at least and devote them to her body, her waist, the buttocks (in what I now know to be a thong as she steps out), the closing of the thighs. And all over again as she stoops for her robe.

But now, suddenly, she catches me. Flashing her eyes, she moves towards me. I stop feeding on her body and cover my eyes. I feel my head forced back and suddenly there are lips on mine, forcing me against a lighting stud. I am shoved away into the tub and by the time I recover I am alone. Panting.

Eventually I take a towel from the pile. In a pane of blue bubble glass I can see two figures running through the garden. I am confused. Not frightened, but uncertain, frigging confused.

"Hello, Jack," says Diana in the kitchen. "How do you like our tub?"

"I like it very much, Diana."

"We thought we'd go to a restaurant tonight, Jack," says Diana. "Should you call your Dad?"

"No need."

I'm still rushing inside as I go up to the room I always use. Nena's door is ajar but I'm not loose enough to do more than rest a finger on the handle. Dan is leaning over the banister above, smiling broadly. I get ready quickly and, for the first time ever, I brush my hair back off my face and apply gel. I am light inside. I need food to weigh down my organs. I smile uncertainly at the mirror. She has said I am good-looking. I need food.

We are seated in the busy restaurant, a place left between Doug and me for Nena who is to join us soon. Chipmunking down the first breadstick, I make a mouth mush of the second with a gulp of cold wine. Dan looks handsome in a dark blue shirt. I feel better now that I'm feeding.

I order gnocchi because I've seen it pass twice and it looks heavy. I take hungry mouthfuls and hope the soft weights will settle my insides.

But now Nena has arrived, in a dress, a small one.

"Darling, you look gorgeous!"

"Thanks, mother."

"For us?" says Doug, raising his eyebrows, taking off his glasses, putting them on. "Is this outfit for us?"

The gnocchi might be so many ping pong balls now. Waiters are waiting – for proud Doug's eye to flick briefly from his daughter whom they also cleverly scope. Why should I be shy any more amidst such general homage? I stare and Dan kicks me.

He goes on needling me. I'm happy to be pricked because I love being beside her. She must have forgiven me for being such an idiot in the tub, or else she wouldn't be stealing *my* gnocchi, raiding my chocolate mousse. Pussy cat burglar, lap from my saucer. Kiss me as hard as you like.

But she gets up and goes before the rest of us. A smooth twenty-something is taking her out, and with her go the diners' eyes, an appreciation of the feast they have enjoyed, so much more than an *amuse-gueule*. The adults see friends who join them for more coffee and we decide to walk home.

In the cool air I calm down at last. This is the first peace I've had since the kiss. I can think about it absolutely. How hard my head was pressed against the stone. The pressure of the mouth, the sudden hot breath. All these things come back to me strongly now. That shove into the tub and my solitude. I see Nena's hair tumbling, the silky cascade, but now I am looking not at her face but my friend's.

"Can I kiss you?"

"Again?"

He leads me into a passageway and against a cold wall he does what every little kid loves to do, sticks his tongue out; what every big kid loves to do, sticks his tongue in. I gasp and then, in my shock, slip past him and run down the street. Dan shouts after me, laughing, "Come back! Come back, you jerk!" but I just laugh and run on. In the taxi my hand goes up to my mouth. But I'm not puking, driver, I'm smiling.

Dad seemed to regard my exams as a formality thanks to Fortuna's preparation. Instead he returned to an older theme late one night during a football match I was sitting through because I wanted to get him off the sofa bed. We both knew now that we communicated better with a windscreen or a TV in front of us.

"Remember my colleague who put his boy through Fortuna, Jack?"

"Yes, Dad. I'd like to go to bed now."

"Well, he also managed to get him some work experience."

"I'm too young."

And how many new experiences was a boy supposed to be able to handle?

"Don't be like that, Jack. You will have a good deal

of time after the exams and it is the perfect opportunity to..."

"Experience the world of work, Dad? Business?"

"I took the plunge without ever dangling a toe. Once you've had a taste you could do a Business Studies course at your new school..."

Did he still not realise I could hustle? Initiate? Organise? I could do whatever business I had to do without any stupid course and if he had paid any attention to my establishment at Chevy Oak he would know as much. He was making me very cross again and it was another half an hour before I got him off my bed.

I walked to the college looking out for kissers. Every adult mouth – except Mum's and Dad's – was now holding some fascination. Couples, especially, interested me as I tried to work out how their lips met, how the noses worked, what that moustache did to her face. In the steam of takeaway coffees, there were graphic displays on the steps of Fortuna.

Mortlake must have kissed fleshily from time to time. The secretary certainly kissed – she made her sour smile with full lips. My Science teacher kissed, urgently I had no doubt, her new nose stud impressing her current partner. The Maths teacher must surely have kissed his missus. Lionel kissed but not often enough to his taste. And there, in through the door, came Dan. He kissed.

We ran off together after class, just caught a bus to Chelsea and fell out at the Town Hall. The house was quiet. I went straight up to his room. He followed in a couple of minutes, by which time I was standing at the top of the stairs, trying not to move as he came up to me.

"I owe you," I said and put my mouth to his. I was visiting him this time and, cleverly breathing and kissing simultaneously, I extended the visit, turning him against the landing wall. With the rest of my body, I exerted a little peer pressure.

With Lionel we were reading 'Julius Caesar' as our set book. We made togas at Dan's, found a chicken carcass in the fridge and ripped it apart, slugging wine while horizontal on the Mexican rug. I chucked up classically in the Fortuna gents before English that afternoon. Lionel was ecstatic when we whipped off our coats to continue the reading in costume. As arranged, Nena delivered some grapes to refresh us in the middle of the funeral oration and swiftly enslaved Lionel.

Did Nena know about us? Things were easier with her now, though she could still neuter me with a glance. It was always dangerous. There was nothing dangerous now in kissing Dan. No-one bothered us. We were both quite alone. I could see now that his family loved him in a minimum-attention way. He was like garden furniture they left out in all weathers and occasionally sat on. But he was tough.

And I was getting to be pretty minimum-attention too. Mum rang a couple of times a week. Dad nosed into my life occasionally, usually putting my snout out.

"Where did you go after class today?"

"Round to Dan's."

"Need I have asked?"

"You seemed to need to."

"I mean where else are you ever these days?" Did he want me to sit under his desk polishing the briefcase? Where else had he ever been except that miserable office? "I bet you can't imagine what it'll be like next year."

"School? I can, Dad."

"It's not so much what you learn as who you learn it with. I have friends I first met..." He named a few of his oldest friends we had heard about on the stairs, being boned and binned by Mum after occasional visits. "You'll make real friends at your new school. Friends for life, a balanced crowd... Not just convenience."

Dan was supposed to call round for me. I rang to say I'd meet him at the cinema instead.

Mathematically and scientifically the game was more or less up, but I was still trapping swarms of metaphors in English and flirting with Dan like a terrier. Lionel kept asking if we were all right. And we were. We were all right, all right.

I see the next month as a sequence of photos, a shuffle of moments which I'd be happy to see clattering into the bin.

First, a picture of Dan and I shouting at each other. I have become convinced I want to break first base, steal them all if I had to, hit a home run with him. I can't think of anything else. As I reach for my bat Dan says he's got some bad news.

"Pregnant already?" I am saying nervously.

"We're going back, Jack... to the States. My parents have got a major, major commission and they can't resist it."

"Stuff them! What about—"

"I'm sorry, Jack. It's right for me too."

"You can't just go."

"I have no choice."

"Don't blame it on them, Dan. You said it was right for you..."

"Well, I got to start thinking about schools – I

mean university. Dad keeps asking me about the future. And I see his point. I need to position myself."

"Position! What? You're going to say business school next, aren't you?"

"Sure, eventually."

"And us?"

"It couldn't work. I'm sorry."

"Sorry about what? We haven't done anything."

The last thing you expect of your one basket of eggs is that it grows wings to fly off across the pond – and a hand with which to whip the carpet from under your feet as it departs. His great US, laid out awaiting him: lovers, opportunities, business; my pissy UK: my sad family and my sad government exams for which I was so utterly unprepared.

Next photograph in the series is the candidate's send-off. Dad is laying a hand on my head and I, respectfully bowing in a final lie, accept his blessing before the first exam.

Then a close-up of my confused and frightened face as, just behind me, an invigilator cuts into the bag of Science papers. Minutes later I mistake a diagram of an ear for a snail and fill out the blank labels accordingly.

The photographer would have needed to move fast for the last shot. Instead of attending the Maths exam I went Underground. When I should have been flicking through geometry, algebra and absurd equations, I was clicking through Boston Manor, Osterley and all stations to Terminal Three.

I run to the desk. They've already checked in. I skid over to Departures and just see her hair as she follows them through. That's the shot, me staring at Nena's departing hair, my hands rising to my face as Dan slips through my fingers.

YOU HAVE ONE HOUR LEFT.

Look at the old school clock. 'In memory of Cyril Hunter'. None of us is going to forget that name. One last hour of your boring old face, Cyril. I'd better get on...

If leaving us created a gap in Dad's life, the surging tide of work had quickly slopped into the space. Even the golf was work, he confessed – especially the golf. I had never known him so consumed by work. I asked him about his morning sweats one evening.

"You really want to know, Jack?" he said.

"Well, yes, Dad..."

"And so you will. Work experience starts the Monday after your last exam! I've cleared it with Mortlake. He thinks it is a marvellous idea... Well *you* could look a little bit excited..."

"I am, I mean..."

161

"I think you'll find this experience an opportunity."

On the day Dad still had lots to say. I stood with my face in his armpit on the tube, sweating now myself into the new suit we'd bought at the weekend. My shirt was too small but he had managed to force the button home and, looking at me over my shoulder in the hall mirror, he had made me promise to check on my tie frequently.

"You mustn't let me down, Jack," he whispered as we pulled on out of Holborn. "It's your introduction to the business world. This can be some real education for you, Jack. If I had had this opportunity at your age I'd—"

"Have done something else, Dad?"

"I'd have had a head start. I'd be further on now..."

I noticed a slight bow to his walk as the first suit clicked by on heels.

"She's a great business brain," he said once she and the last of her followers were clear. "A very capable woman, a great business mind. Big piece on her in this week's..."

"Do you work with her? Is she your boss, Dad?" Is she the one who makes you sweat into your cornflakes?

"Eventually, she is everyone's boss. Except his, I

suppose." He stooped again as we walked unnoticed past another big brain.

"I wondered how long it'd be before I saw you two," said a large, baggy-eyed man in the basement.

"Dougie, this is Jack, my son, he's..."

"On work experience, I heard. Except he's not experienced enough to do any work? And he's too young to mess with anything important. Leave him with me, Martin. I'll work out something."

"This morning's suddenly looking very tight, Dougie. I wonder if you could explain to him a little of what goes on down here."

"Relax, Martin. I'll leave him in no doubt where the real work gets done. Leave him with us."

"He's always so busy," I said when Dad had gone. "Are they all like that?"

"Every one. Even the bosses have precious little time to watch their backs. Terrible dorsal pain in this business, know what I mean?"

"Is Dad..." difficult question, "... respected?"

"There's not much of that going round either. He's a good person but he's not a successful 'personality'. Look at his mileage. He might as well be a frigging pilot. He shouldn't be doing all that still... at his age."

"He sweats."

"Not unusual."

"At breakfast?"

"They sweat at lunch and tea. Come on, let me show you these settlement slips. If we don't sort these by ten fifteen we'll all have something to sweat about."

It didn't take me long to find my niche. My hands were soon tugging out concertinaed papers from the photocopier, another much-abused machine which just wanted someone – anyone – to read its manual. And here I stayed, fed cooling drinks by Dougie, for most of the fortnight, copying slips, refilling the carbon, the usual trouble-shooting. I delighted them by revealing the staple option and soon had them all enlarging and reducing on to double-sided. I barely saw Dad and only got him on the phone once by pretending to be a headhunter which he fell for with powerful gratitude, briefly.

As I was leaving Fortuna a few days later I got the secretary's heavy-lipped smile and was immediately suspicious.

"Jack Curling, I have something for you," she offered, holding out the envelope. I took it and left the building. I needed to witness no climax of jollity from her.

I sat on a bench. A pigeon manoeuvred on a ledge opposite, sticking its arse out over the pavement before shooting the white stuff. I jabbed a finger under the flap and quickly found, amongst the Government guff, my results in English, Maths and Science. I felt very, very tired. These results sent me straight to sleep on that bench. They were that boring.

I knew, upon waking from this fake and frightened slumber, that I should tell Dad. He would not find them boring. But shoulds had all turned to slop and I decided to go home.

Mortlake was crossing the road in order not to have to pass me directly. As he billowed along opposite, his suit tight with flab and wind, I looked up in hope. The pigeon was still there but it was right out of shit.

Back home my mood improved a notch. Smells and vistas and clutter, they all meant something vaguely comforting to me, unlike Dad's flat. I made myself a large sandwich. Mum rang. She guessed why I'd come home. I said I'd prefer to tell her the results in person and, just for the hell of it, sounded pathetically excited. Rosie got back from school but she was in a deep temper about something and I wasn't the one to haul her out.

I wrote Mum a note to say I'd be back soon. I was restless. Journeys helped, arrivals didn't, especially this one. I got to Dad's office at six. His screens off, he was packing his briefcase.

"Hello, Jack. Have they come?"

How did they all know? They all seemed to have heard the ding of the Fortuna microwave.

"Come on, man, tell me!" He was out from behind the desk. He had never called me 'man' before. He approached, hands outstretched, knees working high as if he intended to spin me into some dance of celebration. Just as I decided to run for it he grabbed me firmly by the hands. "Tell me!"

Certain nouns have a self sufficiency, a stand-alone quality which makes any surrounding syntax and further description redundant.

"Crap, Dad, crap."

He looked around to see if we were attracting attention. There was an odd smirk on his face.

"'Crap'? What do you *mean*, 'crap'?" Already he spoke with quiet anger and dropped my hands as if they were smeared with the noun.

"Uh?"

He snatched them up again.

"Would you kindly grade this 'crap' of yours for me, Jack?"

"The only one I didn't screw up was Maths."

"But..."

"Because I wasn't there."

"What? *Not there*?"

"Your dear colleagues are looking interested, Dad..."

He lowered his voice. "Come on, Jack, give it to me! In Science, you got...?"

"In Science I got grade two."

"Top grade's one, isn't it?"

"Goes the other way, Dad. Top grade's seven."

"English? Tell me you did OK *in that*."

"OK, I did OK."

"OK what?"

"Got a four. OK?"

"A four! Oh, Jack." He flung down my hands in order to hold up his face. There was nothing he could say but he couldn't stop himself trying. "I'm so disappointed."

"It *is* disappointing."

"How can you say, just like that? 'It is disappointing'?"

"Your word."

"Actually your word *is* better! Crap!" He hissed the word, still hoping he wasn't being overheard. "And I think I can be allowed some astonishment, Jack. And some considerable disappointment, eh? And what do you mean, you *weren't there* in Maths?"

"I bunked."

"Bunked! I'm having great difficulty sustaining this conversation..." This face-to-face stuff was difficult for us both. "You appear to have wasted a lot of time and a *lot* of money." He was still hissing. He switched on his screen.

"Your money."

"And your time, Jack. Yet another year of education. Your CV is already shot to pieces – and your V's hardly started! Have you told Mum?"

He looked up as he asked this.

"I went home this afternoon."

"So you decided to tell *her* first." He looked back at the screen quickly. "And the Yanks too, I suppose."

"They've gone. I *wanted* to tell Mum first."

He coped with the slight.

"She must have been thrilled."

"I didn't see her."

"What?"

"She was at work, of course. I didn't tell her."

"She *will* be thrilled though, won't she?"

"Why? Because she's got one back, Dad? Because it's one all in the Jack Curling Fuck-Up Cup."

"Don't you speak like—"

"That's how you're thinking though, isn't it?"

"No, Jack. It's not." He was scrolling through a huge document. "And I'll thank you not to tell me how I'm thinking."

"Mr Independent!"

"What?"

"Mr I-don't-need-my-family."

"Shut up, Jack."

"Mr Married-to-my-job." I was speaking louder now.

"Don't—"

"Except this relationship's not working so well either, is it? I know why you sweat in the morning,

Dad. I know why you look so cold by evening and why you scream at the football on TV. It's the knives in your back which they throw for fun – not because they fear you. You're not sweating, Dad, you're bleeding. And they're bleedin' laughing at you."

He looked around for any colleagues still lurking amidst the screens. A woman stood up beyond a partition and smiled sadly at us both. When she was out of sight he lunged for my hands yet again. His smirk had become a kind of leer. He got hold of my wrist but I broke free and backed away, knocking a keyboard off the desk and rocking a monitor.

"I'm simply not listening to this. You are going to get into the car and we are driving to your mother to do some straight talking."

"I thought that's what—"

"About you, Jack, and about your exams. Not about my career and definitely not about the marriage which caused you..."

We didn't say a word to each other on that halting journey through the dark. London's brake lights were splattered against our wet windscreen and I tried to have them hypnotise me.

And when Mum whooped for joy, I thought I must have cast myself deep inside some childish memory, perhaps reliving the moment when first she pressed me to her emptied belly.

"'A' in Maths, Jack!"

"'A' for Absent." And Dad also took it upon himself to explain the others. Her disappointment added to his seemed no longer bearable. I could go either way, implode or explode, and both meant tears – in front of Tommy and Rosie.

"Go upstairs, you two," said Mum and I could have hugged her for that though she'd have cast me aside. Of course I knew just how far upstairs they'd go. "How *could* you do so badly, Jack?"

"That's just what I want to know."

"What were you thinking of?"

"Did you *forget* to revise?"

I put a cushion in front of my face and, such was their harmony, I no longer knew which one was saying what.

"Did you *panic*?"

"What have you got to say, Jack?"

"Yes, let's hear *him* speak!"

"Was this *deliberate*?"

"Do you *want* to throw away any chance of a decent future?"

I eased the cushion off my face to concentrate on the carpet's pattern which was repeated exactly three times in the space between the coffee table's leg and the fake fire's brassy surround.

Dad had been pumping up with pus throughout the car journey, but I was disappointed to find Mum so septic. She knew even less than he did about my London life. Would he bother trying to get me into one of his posh schools now? Did she have any better ideas? Was I now an official school refuser, on the way to becoming a feral child? Maybe I would have to be educated in the home, the ideal home.

"It's hard to imagine more favourable circumstances for study," Dad said, thankfully going just too far.

"Not *that* hard," said Mum, turning quickly with the steel in her cords tightening a notch.

"I mean he only had three subjects to do, Polly."

"Was that a good thing? Better than a balanced curriculum?"

"What *could* be better than one-to-one tuition?"

"Perhaps he didn't get on with the teachers."

"Get on with them, Polly? I was merely asking Jack to learn a teensy weensy bit, not marry them."

"So you're not setting up as a matchmaker. Just a highly successful educational consultant—"

"I tried, Polly."

"Let's get the order right. First you scoffed, later you *ignored*, and only *then* did you try. Jack, you better go upstairs as well," said Mum.

Not before I lobbed in, "Dad thinks I screwed up to get back at him."

"That's ridiculous, Jack! Polly! Look, can we try to stick to the point? Have you got any whisky? I've already told you once this evening, Jack, this is not about your mother and me. You will *not* hijack the conversation which is about how you, Jack Curling, could have done quite so badly in three public examinations for which you have been intensively and expensively coached with a view to getting into a recognised school and finally *doing* something with your life."

Mum snatched back the controls from the hijacker. It seemed whisky would not, in fact, be offered to the passenger.

"I don't think you can imagine what it has been like here over the past six months or so, Martin. Otherwise you could not allow yourself to be so thick and pompous. While you've been massaging rich egos' portfolios, or whatever the hell it is you do, I've been trying to explain to a rather confused but very interested audience what has happened to their 'home'."

"He's been living with me, Polly, that's what's 'happened'. We have talked from time to time but we've both been busy and we've just got on with it. At least I *thought* Jack was getting on."

"And I thought *you* were," I rammed my words in edgeways, one hand on the door handle.

"Go upstairs!"

"Hang on, Mum. I *thought* he was getting on until I had to hang around his pissy office for days on end."

"How dare you!"

He stood up and made a grab at me, same wrist. Missed.

"Martin!"

"Remember, Dad, I *know* why you sweat in the morning," I said around the door. "Mum would know too if you were ever stupid enough to offer *her* work experience."

"Jack, you are going too far. What's got into you?"

"Ask him." I stepped back into the room.

"Damned if I know, Polly. Never heard anything like it."

"You *do* know, Dad."

"Enough Jack. This is getting us nowhere. You're trying to make fools of us all. Really you are. *I'm* going upstairs if you won't."

I sat down. Dad stood as she pushed past me.

"Sit down," I said and he obeyed, glancing at the cupboard. "Mum's chucked the whisky," I said. There was a long silence.

"We had a deal, Dad."

"Did we? When? What?"

"You said if I settled in at Chevy Oak – if I could establish myself – you'd accept it. You would..."

"Would what?"

"Say well done. Be pleased. Accept it!"

"Oh really. What do you mean 'establish' yourself? Does that have anything to do with academics? I think not. What do you mean 'establish' yourself?"

"It was *your* flipping word. And it means exactly what I did. Be happy there. Know everyone. Become well known. Feel confident. Feel quite safe. Get interested in some stuff."

"And you were?"

"I almost was. Definitely, I was happy."

"Well, that's something."

"Is it? You didn't even notice."

Silence. He shifted in his chair.

"Why, Dad? Why didn't you notice?"

"Because, Jack..."

"Yes? She didn't really throw away the whisky."

"Because I was – you must be able to see this – so busy. I knew things weren't exactly happy. I wasn't happy. Your Mum certainly wasn't. But at least I was desperately busy."

"So you talked about it with Mum?"

"No, we didn't talk." So I'd been trying to eavesdrop on silence. "We just considered it, by ourselves, separately."

"And all the time I thought you were watching me."

"Tommy and Rosie will have thought the same. It's a trick parents have to play on their kids. Lasts a bit longer than Santa – at least I hope it does. We were looking out for all three of you."

"Just looking out through curtains, thick 'uns."

"What do you mean, Jack?"

"I wanted to tell you how it all was, Dad, at the end of my second year, as we agreed. I even bought some caviar."

"I see... the caviar. You *bought* some? What with?"

I found myself abandoning words. Quite suddenly I was standing in front of Dad with an imaginary tin, cradling it to show immense value. Then I mimed a frenzied opening of the tin and showed him how it had been that evening: a furious guzzling and slurping up of fish eggs, my tongue jabbing through the tin at Dad. I could taste it now, utterly delicious, despite everything.

Dad looked dumbstruck. He never liked charades.

"I wanted to sit out with you in the garden and put it on the bread for you and tell you how well I'd done. Instead I had to go out there alone and neck the lot."

"When was this?" he asked after a pause. "The start of your summer holidays?"

"The last day of my second year—"

"Which happened to be the evening I finally walked out. Mum never even mentioned it."

"Why should she have? It was nothing to do with her. It was our deal, Dad. She didn't even know about it."

He shoved the chair forwards, got his elbows on his knees. "Our deal, of course it was," he whispered through fingers.

"I had planned for us to tell her about it after the caviar. Then we'd have been together with the whole summer in front of us."

We sat silently for several minutes. I thought about going to bed but I kept expecting Dad to say something more. I flicked my trousers in a kind of nervous encouragement. Eventually he did speak. At the blank television screen.

"You can blame me for a lot, Jack, and I understand why you do. You can blame me for my part in splitting up the family. You can even laugh at what I do all day every day. And of course I feel terrible about our deal. It's every father's nightmare... But I will *not* accept the blame for your exams. And it wouldn't help you if I did accept it. Every one finds his own way up the creek."

At last I couldn't think of anything to say. Perhaps I should have understood, have instantly forgiven, but I didn't. I sat looking at Dad for several minutes. He wasn't looking at me. Instead he got up and walked towards the door. At the last minute he swerved and kissed me in the middle of the forehead.

"I could probably find that whisky, you know."

"Don't worry, Jack. I must be off. Next time. Perhaps."

I hauled myself upstairs to bed. After Mum had come in to give me a hug, I cried. Perhaps, I thought, I wouldn't see him for months now. I also knew I would be finding my own way out of the creek.

I went down to the do-it-yourself store with my old mate Michael to get Mum some wood stain. I was in awe of my loud companion and quite grateful to be by his side. I'd never seen him so sneering and cocky. I felt raw and shaky, too embarrassed even to ask an assistant about the stain. Meanwhile Michael was bowling on ahead down the aisles, touching everything and swivelling his hips at the security cameras.

"Oi, Jack! C'm here!" he shouted from the end of the hanger.

I went towards him, even unsure of my gait and how fast to go. Were these the same feet that had flown me up and down London with Dan?

"Quickly!" he barked and I obeyed. He just didn't care, Michael. When I got to the end of the aisle he grabbed my shoulder and together we peered round the shelves to see Ronaldson examining drills.

"'Ere, watch this!" Michael hissed. He pushed me back out of sight and, shifting some pots of varnish so he had an eye hole, softly trilled, "Ronaldo!"

"Michael, *don't*!" I was not keen to say hello.

So Michael started barking. "Ronny, Ronny, Ronny, Ronaldo." I scuttled down the aisle and looked on from afar as my former tutor turned in surprise. Michael legged it down the aisle towards me, laughing raucously.

" Let's go caff."

"I've got to pay." I'd found the stuff.

Michael disappeared as I joined a queue. I was about to be dealt with when I heard, "This is a customer announcement. Would a Mr Ronaldson, currently shopping, please go to till twenty-seven immediately." Trolleys in front of me, trolleys behind me, I was trapped at 27 – and Ronaldson was prompt.

"Hello, Jack." He looked understandably bemused. "How are you?"

"Fine thanks." We were talking around a large man eager to get off to his grouting. I pulled my stain from the swipe zone and squeezed back, allowing the man through.

"Did *you* call me?"

"Not exactly."

We both saw Michael gesture obscenely from the car park.

"I see him – Chevy Oak's finest. But, how are *you*?"

"All right."

"Shall we have a quick cup of do-it-yourself tea?"

We went through the tills and settled at a table. I told him about Fortuna and about failing everything.

"But I want to know if you're *happy*," he said. "How's Dad? You enjoying London? Friends?"

"You sound like my mother!"

"Sorry. How's she?"

"The same. Bit lonely."

"Tommy seems like a nice kid."

"Yeah? D'you teach him?"

"No, but he's always *curling* around the place, not quite as outrageously as his brother."

"Plays football though," I added.

"Doesn't, does he? I'll have to have a word with him."

"You'll be up against Dad on that."

"I suspect he's not too pleased with you right now."

"He can't decide whether to wash his hands or drown me with them."

"That bad, eh?"

"He's angry now. And so am I."

"About the crammer? Are you going back to Fortuna College?"

"Course not. I wouldn't have it."

"And they wouldn't have you?"

"No. I couldn't give a monkey's. I've had it with schools."

"No, Jack. I've *had* it. Your parents have *had* it. We've had our chances and we've made our choices. We are past our learn-by date. But you're not! You've been treading water for three years – the sort of luxury most people save for college. You've managed to stay afloat. Now you had better start going forward."

"When I just want to sink..."

Michael appeared with an elaborate, "Hello, Sir!"

"I was just leaving, Michael. Nothing to do with you. I am going home now to make large holes in the plaster. I feel just in the mood for a little light destruction. But I want to hear something different from you, Jack, and soon, even if I have to drill down your front door to hear it. Goodbye."

"B-bye."

"What's twistin' his nuts then?"

The next day a letter from Dan upset me. I shook with excitement as I examined the alien stationery on my lap, smoothed dog ears out of the colourful superpower stamps. Said he'd gone straight into school in New York, the one he'd had in mind, of course, and was happy. The city, though, disappointed him after London. Nena was seeing someone who reminded him of Lionel except he had money, banker rather than teacher. Diana thought Doug was having an affair but she was too busy to complain.

And then towards the end of the page he wrote, 'I won't forget those classes in that weird room at the top of the stairs which the sun always reached. I miss you. You are a great friend and I was lucky to run into you. And when we meet again, Jack, I expect to envy you.'

I read it through a couple of times. His confidence still worked on me. He still worked on me and I kept the letter. I kept the envelope. I missed him so much. There was nothing else to do.

Fortunately Mum and Dad pulled in their horns. He went off to Caracas and she was being surprisingly OK. But still I could not relax. Nobbi took me on for a few hours a day. He trod round my difficulties. I couldn't decide whether it was worse to be given lots of advice or to be given none. Time slowed, the free mangoes soured and the blackbird, on a cherry mission, pecked my finger.

Nobbi and I played desultory catch with oranges but I was no competition, couldn't concentrate. Cheerful Tommy occasionally coming by and catching the orange in his pocket without breaking his stride – and with his whole life in front of him – didn't help me one pip.

I was shifting a batch of rotten fruit towards the bins one morning when I saw Ronaldson passing. I ignored a customer to watch him walk all the way to the end of the road. Then I handed over the wrong goods and/or wrong change and, defying Nobbi's shouts, I ran after Ronaldson.

"Sir!"

"Hello, Jack." He looked cool, as in unfriendly.

"You know you said you wanted to hear something different from me?"

"Yes."

"Well, I've been thinking..."

"And?"

"Put it this way – I may decide I want to work for Nobbi, go into greengrocery, eventually. But I want to be in a position to make that decision. In other words I want to get a few exams first."

"I'm glad to hear that, Jack."

"So will you come round to our house, sir? I need some help. I think we all do. We need someone to talk to. Can it be you?"

A couple of days later, it was.

"Welcome aboard, Mr Ronaldson," cried Mum. "Welcome to the SS Chaos!"

I put myself on the tea detail and ripped open some biscuits. When the slurping and snaffling had subsided, Mum hugged her knees and opened proceedings.

"We're very pleased you've come round, Mr Ronaldson. My 'late' husband and I are, well, panicking. He's panicking at 30,000 feet and I'm here. Panicking."

"Do you have any schools in mind, Mrs Curling? Are you thinking about a particular school?"

"I think about nothing else. A friendly, supportive, encouraging school with good results and a nice uniform. I think about a particular school all the time. Except I don't know where it is."

To kill off the silence we needed an airliner, not these chinking teacups – nor Rosie who suddenly offered a passionate critique of modern education.

"I cannot understand why, Mr Ronaldson, you teachers and government people wait all these years before deciding to examine Jack and his friends on every subject under the sun other than sex – when *that* is the one thing they are interested in."

I gulped at my tea and felt the leaf faintly at the back of my throat. They were all looking at me. What did she know?

"Thanks for your sympathy," I managed. "I do feel very embarrassed about school and college at the moment. And I feel very—"

"Angry?" Rosie prompted. Useful umbrella word these days but I wished she'd shut up.

"Yeah, angry... especially about my time at Chevy Oak. I wanted to do well. I did do my best. I thought I had done well. But I couldn't have been doing that well because everything fell apart."

It was as if a pole down Mum's spine had suddenly been pulled out. She seemed to collapse.

"You *were* doing well," she cried. "If I'd ever thought you were in any doubt, I'd have told you again and again. But you seemed so happy."

"I was. I knew Dad hated me going to Chevy Oak but I thought I was doing so well he was coming round to the idea – he must have been – and then suddenly, he just went off."

Tommy was rubbing Mum's back.

"I know. I know," she said quietly. "But I had no idea how you were going to take it. How Rosie, how Tommy would take it but, to be honest, I had to let it sink in here first." She pressed her chest. "And by the time I was ready to ask you – you were telling me in your own way."

Ronaldson raised his hands as he does in class.

"I'm not sure what else I can say except to ask whether you might look at it in a different way."

"I suppose you mean a private school?" Mum sniffed.

"No, no. All I had in mind, rather than looking all over the place for a suitable *new* school, was that you might consider a suitable *old* school, an old school for Jack."

"What?"

"Well, I'd like to do all I can to get Jack back on roll at Chevy Oak for the start of next term."

I stared into my tea. A lone leafy bit had slipped through the net and bobbed bewitchingly in the grey brown. How should I read it? I knew where my future lay. Ronaldson appeared to be quite as sure. He didn't know me now, but he had known what I could have been and he knew what I could yet be.

"The population is shifting. I lost two from my tutor group at the end of last term so they'll be giving me two new faces for sure. Why can't I try to make one of them old Jack – a face we know and like?"

"Do you think you could?"

"I'm sure of it, Mrs Curling. After all, we do have a sibling rule." He nodded at Tommy who seemed chuffed to be saving the day. "But we need to hear from Jack."

"Sir?"

"Am I to run with this or not?"

"Think so..."

"And you won't mess up – getting both of us hauled before the Head?"

"No, sir."

"Even when teachers hassle you because you are behind other kids?"

"Private tutors after school!" cried Mum. "Coaches at dawn!"

"I can get back into the rest, sir."

"You could start a new subject – Business Studies?"

Mr Finch, a grey-beige blur, and Dad, leaking golf balls, cartwheeled together through my head space.

"Do I have to?"

But I think this was the moment when I realised Business Studies was one GCSE I really had to do, and do in style.

"I'll let you know how I get on with the Head," said Ronaldson, getting up.

"Let's hope this works," sighed Mum.

"I've a feeling it will," said Ronaldson. "At least he knows where to come. And Tommy knows when term starts."

"Oh yes," my sibling saviour simpered. "And we'll do all we can to get him there on time."

DO NOT TRY TO COMMUNICATE WITH YOUR NEIGHBOUR. DO NOT TRY TO HIDE UNDER THE PLANE NOISE. WE CAN LIP-READ.

Michael and Razza are both here. They haven't looked exactly busy though, of course, they've been more industrious than me. Warren's sitting in the top corner. A few minutes ago he got a caution for laughing at a question.

I was nervous. Tommy made sure he was walking between me and the skip this time. At Nobbi's he paused for a chat. Both of them were in on it and both tried nicely to coax me into the conversation. So low was my self-esteem that when, quite close to the gates, the little bastard did a run-through of my uniform and equipment, I let him get away with it.

Some of the tougher lads had closed down during my absence which was, frankly, a relief. Their faces, however, had taken off: complexions had been destroyed, noses were now taking a line and eyebrows had joined forces for manhood. They'd stopped all pretence at working.

"Why can't we go on firing spitballs? We was gettin' quite accrit."

"Why does no-one laugh at me farts no more?"

"All rite, Jack? Herd you bin bunkin'..."

The little girls had been replaced by big ones, big girls who were unimpressed that their life circumstances had not developed with their bodies. So there was not much 'Jack's back' enthusiasm from them. Stacey Timms teased me.

"What do you look so jumpy about all the time, Jack? I won't eat you!" she giggled, turning from Razza as she stroked his crotch in Maths. "Don'tcha like us girlies, then?"

Of course the staff were better informed of my situation. "Hey, what *do* you think you are doing?" had become, "*How* do you think you are doing, Jack?" The Head gave me some quality face-time and claimed that Ronaldson would be reporting to him directly and regularly. Ronaldson himself was very exam-oriented these days and made us start each morning imagining thousands of glowing light bulbs around the classroom walls.

"Look," he said, with a little extinguishing gesture,

"They are going out – one for each minute until your GCSEs."

Schuman was very pleased to see me and insisted I use the library "whenever, as a bolt-hole from the madness". Sal looked knackered and, in welcoming me back, admitted the last year had been hard on her too. Culinary Studies had not been awarded public exam status and she was keen to get back to the restaurant business. Ms Grundle was haughty in victory and keen to show that she knew the colours of my 'year off' but she let me be served.

Michael's friendship with Razza had grown highly toxic. They sloped around school emitting poison through their eyes, their lips, the tips of their jabbing fingers. Puffs of the stuff hung in the wake of their corridor swagger, the stink of a new arrogance or desperation.

I didn't want to lose them – especially Michael – because I was afraid of the holes friends can make when they move off. Dan was still in touch. He mailed mementoes of his time in London, sometimes enclosed with letters, mostly not. A bus ticket with 'Where were we going? Why?' on the back; his tube of British toothpaste now finally exhausted; and a photo of the pair of us at the top of a City church. A little out of focus, it had been taken by a fat tourist who had gamely leaned out to get the angle. We had our arms round each other and were smiling like gangsters.

These tokens didn't help. Dan was just a gap in my life and I had to accept the likes of Michael as more real to me now. He and Razza had discovered a pub. Out of their dads' drinking range, it also had pool, which gave new point to existence and focus for their truancy. Easier to get a table early afternoon, I was told. Like a proud spouse, non-playing Michael would sit and watch Razza prod the balls about, very slowly getting as drunk as funds allowed. I know because I went down there.

I was on the bus with a kid called Warren. Ronaldson had quietly suggested I get as much help as possible – in any subject going – from Warren, who had always been super-bright and super-lonely. He took the trouble to remind me of some of my campaigns and he said how much he had enjoyed them.

"You were really safe, Jack, really established..."

That word! I told him quietly that I thought he was probably the more established one these days.

We were going to his place to watch a video of our Eng Lit play. He was asking me whether I had managed to read the whole text yet and I was telling an untruth when Michael barged on to the bus, insulted the driver and plonked himself down three seats up from us.

"It's a very limited film version," Warren was saying in his usual clear manner, "but we should get something from it."

I wished he'd keep his voice down.

"Look, you can see our house." It was next to a convenience store whose name was proclaimed in large letters on a shiny red background: Emporio Tiptop. "That's where I work," he said, moving to the door. But Michael jabbed out a hand as I passed.

"Request stop."

"Hello, Michael."

"Hi Jack. Hi, Wawen," he sneered. "Come for a drink, mate?"

"I'm going, er... Warren...?"

"It's not my decision," he said, clear as a bell. "And it's not yours, Michael. It's Jack's."

Warren got off before Michael could grab him. I hesitated, the doors shut and Michael swore. I looked out, agitated and embarrassed, as Warren simply shrugged and smiled.

"Need to talk, Jack."

"But – where are we going?"

"Pub of course. Razza's there."

"Great."

"Chat over a beer, eh?"

A beer it was. I had to lend Michael 20p for it and make do with some peanuts myself. And with Razza enjoying his game, Michael explained that last year's GCSE papers would be used for the mock exams in March.

"I know, Michael. So what?" Of all the topics for him to select in The Pot and Cannon!

"So that's why we have 'em."

"What do you mean, you 'have them'?"

"We have 'em, Jack, 'cos we thought they'd be handy."

"For what?"

"For the poor sods taking mocks after Christmas."

"You're going to *tell* them the answers?"

"Not tell 'em, Jack. Sell 'em."

"And not the answers." This was Razza, pausing to chalk his cue and show his conspiracy with Michael. "The questions, Jack."

They said they knew of about thirty interested kids.

"What are you selling the papers at?"

"Tenner a basic pack plus a quid fifty for options like Business Studies."

"English Literature?"

"Yeah, yeah. Two fifty. That was hard to get, that was."

"How did you get *any* of them?"

"Most off of that kid, Jed, younger brother of the one who kicked the shit out of you in Year Seven. Well anyway, Jed was really built. Kept walking out of his exams after an hour and he never left his bleeding answer booklet, let alone the questions. No-one was going to get it off him. Told the teacher he'd take his GCSEs outside where he could rip them to shreds in peace."

"Why did he turn up at all?"

"His dad hired this even huger geezer to brung him each day. His dad is the only geezer in Hounslow bigger 'n 'im."

"And you ran into him?"

"By chance the first time. Stacey saw him by the gates, didn'tya, Stace."

She was suddenly there by Razza, moving gently against his cue side.

"He was ripping up History," Michael went on. "In fact he had ripped it up. Clever girl just picked up the pieces. All except one section out of Dictators."

"Hitler must of blown away," giggled Stacey, lighting up.

"It was Starlin'," said Razza.

"And you got his other papers?"

"It was easy after that," Michael continued. "We'd

just get to him while he was beginning to rip each one up or thinking about it, distract him with a ciggy, or say we was interested."

"Coupla times I said I was interested... Know what I mean, Jack?" said Stacey. "*He* seemed to like the idea."

"He didn't care, just handed them over, most in one or just two pieces. He did screw us with one of the Sciences – he tore it up in the hall and chucked it under his desk, the fucker." Michael drew hard on his cigarette.

"So what did you do for that one?"

"Debriefed stiffs! Persuaded them to tell us all what they could remember about that paper. Same wiv' Eng Lit."

"Yeah, and French," said Razza. "D'ya remember that kid scribbling the French? Amazing powers of recall."

"Probably made it up," I suggested.

They turned to stare at me.

"Like he made up his home address?" said Razza. "Leave it out, Jack! We checked on the school records."

"Got in there, have you?"

"Everywhere, mate." Michael paused. "Look at what we're saying here, Jack. Look at why we're saying it to you."

"No idea."

"So as you know we haven't sat still this last year, beating off about the good old days when Jumbo Jack went Beyond The Door with his happy snacks," said Michael.

"So where are all the papers now?" I asked.

"Under my bed. Where they'll stay until the last week of term. Kids always have money before Christmas. What better pressie for the old lady than top marks in mocks in the New Year?"

"And next year, will you be providing the same service when *we* do our mocks?"

"Nosy, in't he?" said Stacey.

"Most certainly we will be providing, Jack. And for ever after. All over London. Purveyors of fine mocks to succeeding generations. Robin Hood – take from the thick and sell to the rich. Sounds all right, don't it?"

"Aren't you forgetting something?"

"Doubt it. Are we, Razza?"

"Unlikely."

"Stace?"

"No chance."

"Mocks are one thing," I said. "But what about the real exams?"

"Jack, mate, it's been luvverly chatting but it's getting near your bedtime and we've got things to discuss... Ain't we, Mike?"

"Cheers, mate. Give Wawen a goodnight sloppy from me, will ya!"

Stacey craned forward, wriggled in her shirt and pretended to want to kiss me. A year is a long time in education, I thought, and quickly caught my bus.

Mum went off alone to Parents' Evening, and came back clucking. The next day Ronaldson confirmed to me that my teachers all thought I was working harder.

"I've told the Head you've started well," said Ronaldson. "You aren't letting yourself – or, more importantly, myself – down! Your parents looked chuffed too."

"Parents?"

"Your Dad was especially pleased with Mr Finch's comments about your Business Studies."

I was pleased to hear this, not only that he was there at all but because Dad needed to have the highest possible expectations of my GCSE result in his sacred subject.

"He told me all about your work experience too."

"I doubt it, sir."

"Well, he's sounding pretty bullish about your future. I'm glad things are sorting out."

In the last week of term, the 'product' was launched amid intense security.

"Busy, Jack, ve-ry busy," was all Michael would reveal.

"How many have you sold?" I asked Razza the next day.

"Oooh, forty or fifty."

"But why don't they just buy one and copy it off each other?"

"No idea."

But Michael knew. "Can I explain the beauty of the plan?" He simply couldn't resist telling me. "Loads of kids get all arsy and serious in Year Eleven. 'Salready happening to you – clutching their heads and telling each other it's the most important year of their lives. So how many of them are actually goin' to admit they've bought the questions?"

"Won't the teachers get suspicious?"

"Maybe. Who cares? But we've sold a few bum steers," said Michael, "to ensure occasional fuck-ups."

"Like we said go big on causes of... what was it, Michael?"

"Causes of the French Revolution, Razza boy. And Worm Reproduction. In actual fact it's the *effects* of the frogs' rev..."

"And fish sex," said Razza.

We were all sniggering when another anguished Year Eleven sidled up and they both disappeared with him into a classroom, flushing out some frightened kids including Tommy. He must have known by now his privileged status as my guardian was dwindling against my growing confidence. But in what direction was it growing?

I was throwing myself wholeheartedly into my work, but I was also preoccupied with Michael's assault on the examinations which underpin the entire school system.

A few days later I did set eyes on the product, though I had to get myself back to The Pot to do so. They were spending more time down there because they had shitloads of cash to shift over the festive season. And, fair play to them, they had done a decent piece of photocopying. For your tenner, you got a pair of heavy duty staples making a wicked little booklet with the blatant slogan 'Just cheat'. Michael no longer had to tease out one or two bottles and had learnt to lock open his gullet to cope with the new plenty.

"I suppose I'm impressed," I said weakly, sucking on a complimentary beer.

"I suppose you should be," said Michael, half-mullered.

We tried – and failed – to talk about something else. A couple more beers made me feel cosier in their company. I thought I might have been touching Stacey's foot under the table but, since she was snogging Razza intermittently, I returned to the subject.

"I still don't get what happens when March moves on to May and June and the sods have to do the real papers?"

"Oh no!" spluttered Razza. "Hadn't thought of that! Had we?"

"Bleedin' hell. You're right, Jack," said Michael. "Keep coming back to this one, don't ya?"

"So what's the plan?"

"Suffice it to say, we have a system in place which – how shall I put it, Razza?"

"Er..."

"Obviates the need for further worry..." said Michael smugly.

"And *ob vee ates* the need for further study!" Razza grinned.

"Freeing us up for ever-increasing Business Studies," continued Michael. "That's the practical money-making side of the subject, not the balls-aching crap you're served up with by Finch."

"Nothing short of a revolution in education as we know it," I contributed. "You pays your money and you gets results?"

"You got it, Jacky boy. Pork scratching?"

"Makes a change from rock cakes, don't it?" taunted Stacey.

I walked out of The Pot enjoying the cool, fresher air, free from their thievish arrogance and the temptation I knew they were dangling. I tried to calm myself by thinking of the still-life I was doing in Art of a buckled number plate sticking out of a cow's skull. It did actually look like a halfway convincing roadkill and the teacher said it would make coursework. Buses passed and still I was walking. A plane went across the brief dark and orange sky and I wondered, as always, whether Dad was looking down from it, eavesdropping on my life. Eventually I gave chase to a bus which let me on outside the Emporio Tiptop. As I took a seat I looked into the shop. Warren was having a laugh with a fit-looking Asian girl surrounded by cardboard filmstars in the video section.

GCSE mocks came and went for the year group above us and, after Christmas, it became clear they had scored a record number of juicy grades. Bumcheeks clutched himself with delight at assembly as he honoured the most successful of his aubergines. I tried not to look at three particular chairs in my tutor group, whose occupants were unusually perky. Eventually Bumcheeks himself noticed them, picking on –

"Michael! Yes, you! Stand up." He liked to name non-listeners in assembly. "I think you of all people should listen to this. Next year…"

Michael stood up, his shoulders at one insolent slant, his sneer at another. When the Head had finished he slumped into his seat with, "Whatever, Bumcheeks," clearly audible at my end of the row where I sat with Warren.

Personally I was growing more interested by the conveyor belt of facts, ideas, theories that was going past our noses every day. I was beginning to think I could have something to show for my efforts. I became more inquisitive about all sorts of subjects. I began wondering, for example, if I shut my oesophagus in the front door at home whether I would have enough guts to reach Nobbi before I twanged back along Rockenden Road. Warren adjudicated here saying that an average bloke like myself wouldn't reach his elastic limit till the main road. But I wanted to show him I was gutsier than that. I began masticating facts and pushing them down with my well-functioning peristalsis. Napoleon, refraction, onomatopoeia, le sobjonctif – I wanted to understand them all. You might as well.

But alongside this conveyor belt ran Michael, shouting distractions in the hope I'd give it all up. At least that's the way I read his pestering and I still did not yet feel safe enough to give Michael up entirely. They had cleared £200 at least – some said half a big one. And were busily investing it – divesting themselves of it – in The Pot.

Knowing this, Ronaldson was worried too.

"They aren't going to get a thing, Jack," he said, extinguishing imaginary bulbs. It was, increasingly, his nervous tic. "I've told Michael it's perspiration not inspiration..."

"They don't *want* to pass, sir. It's not interesting to them."

"But can't you interest them? You've got *yourself* interested. That was at least as much of a challenge as getting Michael going. He's not stupid."

"Razza is."

"But *you* should help Michael. You are still friends?"

"I suppose so, sir, but I don't see much of him."

"Talk to him. Tell him it's urgent – I can't believe how casual kids can be about these bloody exams."

"Oh no, sir, he knows exactly how important they are. He just has his own way of... handling them."

"Well can't you persuade him your way is better? I remember warning you all about his uncle Denny. Every year group has its Dennys. I've seen these guys walking around on the streets – outside school, afterwards, when people don't care about them any more – and the twinkle in their eyes, Jack, it has gone. It goes out with the confidence, just like that, on the day of their results."

"I'll try." But I knew Michael was aiming at very different futures, based on ever-twinkling eyes and ever-jingling pockets.

Still I felt responsible. We had shared so much. I'd outshone him through the first two years at Chevy

Oak but we'd remained friends. Then we had both had a rough year, what with him having to make do with Razza, and me with the full works. But now I was back and ready to help him on to the next stage as requested by Ronaldson. No longer helpless. I could be helpful. I should be.

That very evening Michael was waiting for me outside my house. Out of his uniform he had clearly put on weight and was now *smelling* of pub. Mum was one of the few adults he'd said he could stand but then he hadn't met her for a while and I was quite relieved she was still at work. I fixed us flat colas and we went upstairs.

"So what's happening?" I asked, sitting on my bed as he pushed things around on the desk. An essay, the splayed cover of an all-American baseball just in from NY. I was anxious he should not find Warren's scholarly message on the back of one, Dan's purpler prose on the back of the other.

"Anything wrong, Michael? Haven't seen you around."

He moved from the desk and sat on the floor, back to the door.

"Haven't *been* around, mate. Not school anyhow." He was sizing me up, I could tell.

"So how's – the pub?"

"You taking the piss, Jack?"

"No, mate. Just must get a bit boring, you know, after about ten hours in the pub."

"If you think it's boring chattin' up girls, playin' pool, gettin' meself felt up, gettin' high and bladdered – if you don't like the sound of *that*, Jack, then maybe we ain't got a lot to say to each other no more."

"Maybe, Michael."

"Fact is, Jack, I've had my doubts about you for a long time now. 'Swhy I was waitin' for you. To see, once and for all, if I could find the Jack of old."

"Really. Tell me about these doubts of yours, Michael."

"See, you're taking the piss again, in't ya!"

"No, Michael. I want to talk to you too. We're still mates. We've just changed a bit, that's all."

"You've changed, you mean. Used to have a laugh, Jack."

"Yeah! It was nothing *but* laughs."

"That was all right, that was."

"Still is. But don't you want to do something other than laugh, Michael?"

"I'm doing what I want to do. I've always been independent, a one-off, me. Don't matter to *me* when *my* old man runs off."

"What about your mum?"

"She never stops moaning anyhow so what's the point? I've always wanted cash and now I'm getting it so why shouldn't I enjoy? And them other benefits! You're just jealous, you baaastard." The lengthy vowel persuaded me he was still being friendly though he was definitely getting more difficult to read. "In'tya? Jealous Jumbo Jerk!"

"Can't you see why I am not jealous?"

"There's nothing *to* see except a slimy turd what's turning greener every second." He punched me affectionately, but hard, on the shoulder.

"I don't give bollocks for your rotten money, Michael. I'm not jealous."

"Why not? Don't you *want* money? You think you're better than me, don't you? You think you're superior. I've seen you hanging round the English Department with that little stiff Wawen and the Science Office, chatting up the lab technicians..."

"I've got to catch up, Michael."

"And you probably think five hundred quid ain't worth having. There's *teachers* who'd give anything to get their hands on that kind of money. Where's all their poxy learning got them? It's not about catch-up, mate, it's about overtake and gob-out-the-window after."

"Five hundred! Have you really got that much?"

"Well, we *had* five... Bit less now."

"A lot less, I guess."

"But it'll start coming in again soon. That's business! Cash flow, beer flow! You watch!"

"I will, Michael. What's next? Mail-order drugs?"

"I was going to tell you but..."

"But?"

"You went an' turned into a tosser."

"You don't trust me, do you?"

"Nah. Nah, that's it! I don't no more. I don't trust ya."

"Well you should!" I shouted, definitely not confused about this. Michael should absolutely trust me. I was suddenly angry. I drank some more cola and took deep breaths as I'd heard Mum do after the split. It didn't work for me any better.

Over the next few days I avoided Ronaldson because I felt I had failed him. And I had failed Michael, who obviously had no respect for the new me.

But a week later came his call for me again, after school, through the letter box – my last chance.

"Comin' out, Jack, mate!"

We walked and he talked and we walked some more, eventually passing the mosque and emerging into my old council playground which had been done up and now lay empty. I headed for the swings. In the cold wind we leant into the swinging motion and were soon going well high, forcing metallic protests from the hinges and seeing into first-floor windows. And now, going back and forth, never entirely in time, we returned to the subject of trust.

"Jump!" Michael suddenly shouted.

"Don't be stupid!"

"It's all right. You'll reach the grass! You'll be fine! Jump, Jack!"

"No. No way."

"I'm gonna..." he yelled.

"Don't, Michael!"

"Too late, chicken! Aaaaaaaaaaaaah!"

He sailed off the seat, jacket billowing and landed, just as he said he would, on the grass. That was a jump. He rolled over on to his back and pedalled his boots in the air triumphantly. I slowed.

"There's a shipment coming in," he said, returning to his swing, and building up speed once more.

"This sounds like a bad video, Michael. What are you talking about now?"

I accelerated.

"Listen, willya? They start arriving next month."

"What do?"

"The papers!" I still wasn't there. Then, suddenly, I remembered we were school kids sitting on swings, just getting them going, and there could only be one 'papers' in his mind.

"Supply and demand, Jack." He bucked to and fro on his swing, gaining momentum. I was doing the same. An excuse not to talk. "You build up a client base. They make further demands on you. You strive to supply."

"Supply what?" I uttered in a weak gasp.

"What d'you think?"

"This year's GCSE papers to this year's candidates?"

He was swinging higher and faster than me, his head nodding furiously. "You're *there*, man!"

"You *have* to be joking. Tell me it's a joke, Michael..."

"I cannot, cannot, cannot!"

I was swinging higher now as if trying to catch him up and pull him back to earth. My head was shaking.

"This is crazy," I shouted across at him.

"Jump, Jumbo Jack! Jump!" he yelled and flew off a second time.

This time I had to. I landed next to him – and in that moment I told myself I'd stay next to him for as long as it took to stop this Icarus crap once and for all.

We went over to a bench where I listened to some detail and realised that unfortunately he had been applying some of his intelligence to the heist. Razza had said his dad was a janitor of habit and those habits could be worked around.

"He has every key," Michael smiled. "It's so simple. We just whip one paper out of each box, make up our funpacks and we're in the money again. Except this time they'll be paying ten times as much."

I took a deep breath before killing off the scheme.

"Do you think the exam boards are as stupid as you? They *control* the numbers of papers sent. They have teachers who are *examination officers* in each school who are paid just to count the exam papers in and count them out. You can't get away with it, Michael. Sell drugs, yoyos, anything – but *please* forget this idea."

"You're right, Jack."

"Thank God."

"That's why I knew I had to talk to you."

"I'm glad you did, mate. I really thought you'd lost it."

"Razza's useless like that."

"What? Thinking?"

"And you can help us with the copying as well..."

"What?"

"*Of course*, as you say, we can't run off with the *originals*. We must remain *on location*, you know, open up the library, get you whizzy whizzy with the old photocopier and then seal down the boxes after."

"Did you *hear* me, Michael? Am I hearing you?"

"I hear you, Jack. But listen up. We are having trouble discovering who's the exam officer for next term, who they gets sent to. I put Razza in charge of getting the information because, well, I don't talk to teachers no more – as you probably know. Trouble is Razza and Stacey have stopped talking to them an' all and no matter how many hints he drops his old man can't be arsed to find out for us."

"I'm not *listening*. I'm going now. I've heard enough. I'll tell you one thing though – it's a good job you *can* trust me. But if this is the way you are going don't *ever* think you can count on me."

I made to leave. He was smiling to himself and then transferring it to a girl who had arranged herself on the roundabout and was muttering some enticing abuse.

I felt sick and breathed deeply again as I tripped my way home. There I was pleased to find Mum though I went straight to my room to think. About how I could satisfy Ronaldson, my benefactor, by helping Michael, my misguided mate. What a campaign! I was sure that Michael's plan was doomed, that in overreaching himself he would fall and fall and fall. I had to go along with him now. If he wasn't going to take a hint, then I needed to be there to limit the damage.

Michael was in school the next day as I knew he would be – for market research. It helped my report to Ronaldson.

"We talked," I said. "He is working, sir. It's just things are... very tough, you know, at home."

"All the more reason for getting out and coming in. I'll speak to him at the end of the day."

So, it was going to be no more softly softly from him. I told Michael he'd drawn attention to himself and that he could only hope to succeed if he was working from inside the school. He gave me yesterday's arrogant smile.

"It's hardly going to help if you are excluded or worse, is it?" I persisted.

"What about our exams officer, Jack?"

The sad thing was – and I won't deny it – I was happier, being counted on, being involved in something, anything. Peer pressure, the gripped hand or the barged shoulder, was still better than any pat on the head from a teacher. "Have you discovered yet?"

"Are you going to give me a chance?"

"And once you was so slick..."

I'm sorry to say that got to me. Within the hour I had discovered from Mr Schuman that a certain member of staff was being paid £1009 per annum, before tax, for the honour of distributing and collecting Chevy Oak's examination papers. Meanwhile they would be stored somewhere in the school by that someone.

"It's an outrage that such 'work' is so rewarded when I am simply given reprographics to do – for nothing!" he ranted as we stared out over my runway.

"And I suppose it goes to some senior teacher who hardly needs the cash," I prompted.

"You would think so. Usually does. But this time it has gone to little Mrs Carew."

The one teacher I had not had dealings with since my return – probably because I had had enough for the pair of us before my departure. My only observation since then had been that she'd got pretty fat, an observation confirmed when I 'happened' to meet her in the corridor later. I thought a corridor was safer if she was going to be unpleasant.

But she was a sport from the start, remembering only the good times in the jungle. It seemed elle ne bore pas des grudges. Other things occupied her, it seemed, like a foetus, and she was only too happy to let me relieve her of her load of exercise books.

"He owes you a lot, I think, Jack," she said as we walked towards the Modern Languages office.

"How do you know it's a he?"

"Mr Carew owes you!"

"What?"

"All of us take a bit of time to find our niche in life, eh? And he was never going to be a teacher. But he's going to make a good lawyer, you know. And a good father."

We could hardly move in the office for boxes and Mrs Carew sweetly confirmed for me that it was a major priority for her to get them moved.

"Can I help?" I asked, wondering how far I could go. Perhaps she would let me be off with the papers right away.

"No, no! I've asked George three times already to get them off to the safe. Exam papers are supposed to give *you* a headache, Jack, not me."

"Don't worry, they do."

Michael was horribly pleased with my work. The part of me which should not have revealed my findings was expertly beaten up and silenced by the part of me that I was trying to leave behind. And Michael was revoltingly smug when I asked him about his work, but I had to know now exactly what was happening.

"Oh there's interest, Jack. There's definitely definite interest. Not so much as with the mocks yet... but it'll come, believe me."

"People like who?"

"Jimmy Bradby. Sox Ellis. Kelly Burton. You know the sort."

"The prats who've pissed around for years but don't have the guts to mess up their GCSEs?"

"It's not guts and they're not prats, you prick. They realise our method makes perfect sense."

"Where'll they get the money?"

"That, you don't ask. *Ever*. Let's get it quite clear. Even *I* don't ask that, Jack."

"They'll pay up front?"

"Course."

"Customised shopping lists?"

"Course. Wang Fooey don't want to be paying good money for Science in Gujurati, do he?"

"Right, so you get a copy of each and then you make up individual packages afterwards..."

"Exactamente." Michael seemed to be cheerfully back on task. And I could see that there was something beautiful about providing a stapled sheaf of papers to a client with just enough time to get a few useful answers sorted. A beautiful saving in terms of revision – and skin.

Again there was the arrogant smile.

"Don't get me wrong, Jack. I've nothing against knowledge and learning per se – I used to quite like History, especially those nifty Egyptians."

"That was Primary, Michael."

"So?"

"Was that the last time you were interested in school work?"

"They used to give us chocolate for our hieroglyphics, d'you remember? And them monks who worked on illuminated manuscripts! Book of Kells, that's something

I'd like to investigate fully. I'm just saying I'm not against learning as such so long as it's really targeted. I never could get enthusiastic about stuff we only *might* need. I have got a problem – a big problem – about having my time wasted. It's nothing short of child abuse."

"And are you against having your mind trained?"

"Spoon-fed, Jack, not trained. Spoon-feeding is what they offer here – but smart babies only swallow what they need. Uncle Denny agrees. In fact he has given us his express blessing and wishes such a facility had been thought up before."

"Great. But remember Ronaldson wants to see you at the end of school, Michael."

"Smart babies don't need the likes of him, neither. But me old girl does need twenty-four hours' notice as Ronaldson well knows. And we ain't got twenty-four hours, as *you* very well know. We go in tonight."

As if by horrible black magic, Razza and Stacey joined us.

"Tonight?" I gasped.

"Nice one, Michael," said Razza.

"Makes me feel like a proper scholar," said Stace with a writhe. "Taking me GCSEs early!"

I walked home for some tea. Warren was standing at the bus stop. I crossed the road to avoid him. His all-brands diet of facts amazed me. He was voracious, bolting through the extension work he was now provided in all subjects with a kind of greedy calm and the odd delighted grin. Ronaldson had always said the hard workers would be laughing by the time GCSEs arrived and I think Warren was more amused than ever. I envied him.

HALF AN HOUR LEFT. NO-ONE WILL BE LEAVING EARLY SO, IF YOU FINISH, PLEASE CHECK YOUR SCRIPT. AND AGAIN. AND AGAIN.

Razza had assured us that his dad, George, was in a foul mood.

"Always is, come exams."

I'd heard George myself, out by the bins. "You don't catch senior management puttin' out the fuckin' desks, do you? Heavin' friggin' exam papers around for that uppity little vixen Carew? It's a numbers game to them, Jack, as many bums as possible on as many seats and they think they've got a good school."

At half past six the heist squad met down at the shops and we each chipped in to buy the monstrous pizza which Razza said would finally clog George into complete inaction.

"This can be the birthday present I never got him! And Mum's happy if she don't have to do his tea. If it's

something nice he always eats *before* he locks up."
Which also meant a delay on the nightly setting of
the alarm. Cradled in Razza's arms, the pizza was a
truly sickening sight, grease blotching through its box.
Set me thinking of a murderer's bloodstained vest. By
the time the mozzarella dries out, I thought, the
crime will have happened.

Stacey joined us – dressed in black to the tips of
her clumpy heels. And we walked, guilt in my every
footprint, towards the 'site supervisor's residence'
which lay cosily inside the school gates. I ducked
behind a plant on seeing Mrs Carew being collected
late by hubby in a sports car. I'd happily have let him
run me down. But she spotted me and smiled sweetly.
I felt sicker.

Razza went into the house to establish George's
face well into his teatime treat and then ran out to us
with the bunch of keys wrapped in a cloth. He was
revoltingly excited, clearly the type of criminal who
screams abuse and shakes with adrenalin throughout
the job.

"He won't be out the other side of that in an hour,
greedy bugger. Extra pepperoni and olives – with
their stones left in for extra fiddliness."

We were running round to the back of the school,
past the laboratories.

"That's probably the most intelligent thing you will ever do in your life, Razza," I mentioned. "Leaving the stones in."

My words surprised me, made me think I was even more nervous than I'd realised. Surprised Razza too. He skidded to a halt and shoved me against the wall. The keys and Stacey's index finger dug into my chest as Razza and I faced each other.

"Say that again."

"Leave it, Raz," said Michael.

"Nah! Nah! Nah! I want to know what this tosser said. He's had it coming and I want to hear it again before I let him have it."

"And I said drop it, mate!" Michael flung him off me. "We've got a minute less than we had, we've got shitloads to do and you two are going to work together until we've done it. Then and only then, when we've got our precious GCSEs, will I let you beat the crap out of each other. All right?"

Then, suddenly, all was marvellous. We piled inside, locking the door behind and bowled along the corridors. Michael administered a ringing slap as we passed the fire extinguisher I'd clung to as that bullied new boy. I had to admit it was cool to be there, in control of the empty school, with access to every nook.

Razza opened the Modern Languages Office and handed Michael the torch. There were twice as many boxes in there now. I felt sick again. Mr Carew's mug grinning from his wife's pinboard didn't help.

"You go open the library with Jack," said Michael, pointlessly pulling on his balaclava.

"I'll come up in a minute," I said, suspecting I wouldn't have to turn the photocopier on at all because I'd be needed down here much more immediately. For I believed that, from somewhere, the first set-back of Michael's life of crime would rear up, and that I was here to help him handle it.

He and Stacey were unpiling some boxes which they then started delicately opening. Michael consulted a crumpled sheet of paper which he smoothed flat on Mrs Carew's desk.

"Me shopping list!"

"Ah. Nice," I said.

My heart raced. This had to stop going so well.

"We've got to get a total of twenty-two different papers, get them upstairs, copied and get them back here."

"And boxes sealed down? How are you going to..."

He produced a heavy duty stapler and thick tape. "Razza's eye for detail, mate."

"Hope he has."

"Glad you're here, Jack?" He gave me a smile of real affection, just as he stooped in front of a box. "Let's have a go, Stace. Pass us the knife." Delicately he nicked the lid open.

"There!" He looked up at me again. "Remember what Ronaldson says about GCSEs? He's wrong. It's one per cent perspiration and ninety nine per cent inspiration, eh Jack? What d'you say? Come on, man, relax. Enjoy Maths One."

Michael rose into a kind of slow dance, using the blade as a sort of microphone, gyrating above the boxes, his conquests.

"The beauty of pure Maths," he moaned. "The joy of Eng Lit. The loveliness of the Welsh Board's Science. Come on, Stace, let's dance."

Stacey was happy to make a rocking thigh sandwich with Michael now – and sneaky enough to disengage just before Razza's return, kissing him aggressively on Mrs Carew's desk. Impatient Michael interrupted them to pull her into some more dirty dancing. Razza decided against making a fuss, and then for a few seconds danced with them in a threesome around the blade which Michael held aloft.

I cleared my throat noisily.

"Yeah, all right, Jack, let's get to it," said Michael,

hunkering down over the first open box and pulling at the contents.

It was the last calm thing I heard him say.

"So what now?" I said as he turned the package of papers around and around his hands. It was soundly sealed in heavy duty polythene. The polythene, that was it! My instinct had found physical form.

"It's... it's *shit*!... they're sealed – they're sealed, Jack!"

"In a *fucking condom*!" cried Stacey.

"Have you, er, got a soldering iron in your tool box?" I asked Michael.

"A soldering... course I bloody haven't!"

"So how are you going to seal these up again?"

"Shut up! Shut up! Shut up! Razza, you never said nothing about condoms."

"His eye for detail couldn't see through cardboard I suppose."

"He told you to *shut up*!" Razza snarled. "Let us think!"

Michael, though, was beginning to gibber. "I mean they've never been in bags before – all them past papers..."

"... Were *past* papers, you mug. These ones are unpassed," I said. "They are present – I mean future papers. Virgins. Virgins in condoms."

"Well they ain't going to stop *me*." He shook the package with a vengeful fury. I had to be quick.

"What about this? Will this stop you?" I showed him a cover sheet through the polythene bearing an official warning that any papers opened before 9.15 on the morning of the exam would be immediately invalidated.

"So?"

"Touch one, Michael, and you screw up the whole box."

"I don't believe that."

"You'd better! These are rules. If there's one load of people who are suckers for rules it's teachers."

"Can't we just do a little slit in the bag?" asked Razza.

"You're even stupider than I thought," I said.

"No-one's gonna notice," said Razza.

"You tosser, Razza. I swear Mrs Carew will notice every time. Think about it. She'll pull the packs out of the box before the exam and, even if the whole lot doesn't burst out over her feet, *she's going to notice*. Accept it! Mrs Carew will see and Mrs Carew will have to cancel the whole exam. And when they find one tampered with they'll look out for others and then the board will be called and their detectives and inspectors will come piling in and say the bags were sealed and checked and inventoried when the security trucks left Examination Towers and that they've had no other complaints from any other school and so it's an internal problem and they're very sorry but all candidates will have to retake at Christmas or next summer."

"I told you to *shut up*!"

"He's got a point, Michael," said Razza.

"So? So let's do it!" said Michael, hardening.

"Do what?" we asked together.

"Slash the condoms and the boxes. Let's waste this office. I hate Mrs Carew and her fucking verbs."

"What? You can't be serious." My tone was imploring. I was losing this guy – though I seemed to have gained Razza. Stacey, too, was listening to me now.

"I am serious! I owe it to me clients," Michael continued. "I've taken five hundred quid off them and they deserve something for their money."

"Like what? Cancellation of the exam for the whole school? Razza's dad sacked?"

"Gives them some breathing space, gives me time to think of something..."

"Well think of this," I said. "Think of the hundred kids who *aren't* your clients. Are you prepared to screw their lives too with your little knife?... Well *are* you, Michael?"

In answer, he lunged at the Maths package and dug his fingers into the tough polythene. I stood up and shoved his shoulder hard so he rocked into the filing cabinet, tripped and sprawled across four or five other boxes. Maths One, hundreds of bastard equations, I rescued just before puncturing.

"Put it back in the box now." I tossed the full condom to Razza, testing him as Michael struggled back up. I didn't really believe Michael would slash me but was still happy to toe the knife way under Mrs Carew's desk. Razza buckled nicely and was working in his new cause with great energy. He had already closed up the Maths box and was just taking a length of tape from Stacey when Michael punched me in the face. Hard.

I've seen so many fist fights in films and they've never had any similarity to school fights. When kids like us fight we should start breathing very fast, swinging rounded punches which peter out by the time they connect – with an ear or the back of a head.

Michael's punch though was filmic. It smacked me in the jaw, lifted me off the ground and laid me amongst Combined Science. Realising he had some more medicine for me, I looked up at the door and said desperately, "Hello, Mrs Carew."

Corny, I know, and Michael barely flinched. Barely. And into that naked, unguarded moment I poured all my strength, hefting Media Studies up into his gut. I sprang and held him down.

"Razza! Pull this mother off me! Razza!"

But Razza just made the delightful sound of tape being unwound. I suppose he suddenly feared for his old dad's future and wanted us out without repercussions as soon as possible. Michael though was still crazy for repercussion and the hands at the end of his pinned arms flailed at boxes, tearing at them with stubby fingers.

"I think we're doing the right thing," said Stacey, holding down the flaps of another box for Razza.

"Listen, Michael..." I sat high on his hot chest, Rodeo Jack. "Think about the choice. We can put this room straight and go home. Or we can wreck it and wreck everything for everyone, especially ourselves."

"Or," said the Bronco with a powerful buck. "I can carry on beating the shit out of you." He elvissed his hips and I was flung over and across his face so that my head smashed into a filing cabinet. He kicked me hard in the back of the thigh, pulled me up by the hair to boot me in the chest. Next he picked me up by the head which, going by the sort of movies he watched, I could expect to have pounded again and again against the wall.

"Razza!" I shouted. "Razza mate!"

He looked up from his box work. Perhaps he thought we'd simply cancel each other out. Rather than offer any help, he carefully moved the desk back into line and picked up the fallen telephone. Stacey neatened up the Modern Languages boxes.

Meanwhile, despite Michael's firm grip on my hair, I ran at the wall and halfway up it to launch myself backwards at him, horizontally. I scored a kind of reverse head butt into his chin. Again he got up, finally ripping off his ridiculous balaclava for a punch exchange which made my mouth bleed. He seemed quaintly shocked by this and, into that differential, I darted a jab to blacken his eye and send him down.

"Get out!" sobbed Razza. "Please get out! We gotta put her room back. My old man don't need to lose his job because of bloody us."

We rolled through the doorway, grabbing any bit of each other we could find and continued our struggle in the corridor. Fight! Fight! Fight!

As we made our messy way to the exit, I remember Razza dabbing up drops of blood from floor and locker with his cuff and then the rest of his shirt. Finally Stacey unlocked the back door and we tumbled out into the playground, where Michael gave me back a black eye.

Exhaustion, the fresh air and bloodied Razza's constant reminders that old George, now well olived and mozzarellaed, would be up any minute, served to separate us. My heart was going so fast I was certain it would pump all remaining juice out of my abrasions but I could still run. We passed the site supervisor's house just in time to hear a long belch from George, emerging at his doorway. Michael and I threw ourselves over the school gate and ran off – in opposite directions.

It's difficult running fast with a hand over one eye. It's difficult getting your money out for the bus driver who makes no allowances for blood oozing between your fingers. It's difficult to persuade the caring drunk across the aisle that you don't want to borrow his handkerchief. But I was quite sure all this was much easier than going home to Mum.

I pushed my bruises back into the seat and smiled, even as I noticed the badly cracked face of my Vancouver watch. I was confident that Razza's rearguard housekeeping had covered our tracks and that the papers were still airtight. An evening devoted to a bunch of Year Elevens I hardly knew – candidates who would never appreciate their debt – an evening defending a principle – but more than anything else, an evening dedicated to an old friend. An ex-friend.

I got off the bus to find myself outside the Emporio Tiptop. Warren didn't seem to be working tonight. But I could buy plasters there. It was just a matter of finding the chemisty bit. Was my eye closing? I touched an alien hood of – of me, which had taken awful new shape. It was easier to look down, away from the lights at terrible bottom-shelf vegetables, dehydrated sticky tape and caravan magazines. With a straightening of my spine I had just managed to spot cotton wool and bandages when I noticed a large pair of trainers pointing my way. They moved to block me as I tried to shuffle round.

"I don't think you'll find what you want in here," said a powerfully-built Asian gent. "Whatever it might be."

"But I thought you sold everything." As I really couldn't look him in the eye, I was trying to persuade his trainers.

"We do – but not to everyone. Now go, you young ruffian. Go!"

"I only want some plasters..."

Behind him there appeared slim feet in beautiful Indian slippers. Slim ankles too. Bangled.

"What is it, Ravi?"

"Nothing. Absolutely nothing." But he spoke without his previous assurance.

"Nothing? Nothing? Ravi, have you forgotten your humanity? This is not nothing! This is a poor injured boy..."

The ankles jangled forward.

"Sunita, this is stupid, there are proper customers..."

"Serve them then, Ravi! I will deal with this one." She shot one last glance at him before transferring her attentions. "What happened?" she was asking, smoothing my hair and dabbing at a wound with cotton wool skilfully plucked from an economy bag punctured with her long dark-painted nails. Before I could answer there was another face and another pair of feet, another pair of even slimmer, prettier ankles, in blue heeled boots peeping from behind still present Ravi.

"Laila!" he said. "Please go to your room!"

But this Laila, whom I'd suspected of chatting to Warren in the past, she stayed.

"Darling, can you help me?" Sunita's breath was a sweet, healing balm on my face. "We're going to need a bowl of hot water, Laila."

"Pah! This is madness. I want this youngster, this bloody youth out of my shop in two minutes."

He returned to less bloody customers and I was spirited past rolling ranges of salty snacks and between towers of videos to be helped into a back room and up on to a rusty coffin freezer.

"Oh Mummy. This is no place to nurse."

"Very well. Your room – but there will be ructions..."

We were off again, down a narrow corridor, up some narrower stairs to be laid, finally, on a bed in a room above the shop entrance softly lit by the neon sign hanging directly outside. It seemed a much better arrangement.

These two beautiful females spread me out on the bed, the Tiptop's alternating neon light playing on their skin, red Indians, blue Indians, as they moved back and forth. At any time this would have been a fantastic turn of events but tonight, after my tussle with evil, this had a justice, a heavenly rightness about it. I raised myself up to enable Laila's clever fingers to get at my ripped shirt and tug it off my back.

On Sunita's face a half smile, of concentration perhaps, as she dabbed at newly revealed wounds. On Laila's, intense seriousness as she fulfilled her duties and suggested others for her mother's approval. But just as she had finished with my forehead (and flicked an ear to see it was still attached) I caught her eye, as mine hobbled round her face, and she broke into a beautiful smile which outflashed the neon. My aching body electrified and my heart flipped.

I thought I'd got to my room unnoticed – and into bed – but Mum opened my door to tell me that Razza had rung several times. When I was left alone I began to unwind all but a few of my wrappings. I slept well, dreamed sweetly and awoke with a story for Mum about how I'd been sprinting home up Rockenden Road when I'd collided with the skip.

Ravi and Sunita were having an animated conversation by the dairy fridge when I got there. Laila looked furious behind the video counter. Not a happy shop. Only Warren was cheerful, and I hadn't come to see him.

"I didn't know you knew Laila," he called after me.

"Hello, Laila." I went over. "Anything wrong?"

"You apparently."

"What?"

"Except it's not your problem, it's theirs. They just have to see you at the door and this happens. Mummy is now trying to prevent Pappa from throwing you out."

"I see... And you?"

"Fed up. How are those bruises?"

"As good as gone. Honestly. I just came to thank you."

"It was nothing. I mean not exactly nothing. It was interesting. About the most interesting thing that's going to happen to *me* for a while anyway."

"I bought you this."

Her eyes widened with pleasure as I discreetly teased a mango out of my pocket on to the counter. Mangoes buff up nicely if you stroke them briskly on the lining of your pocket.

"Thank you."

"My name's Jack Curling, by the way. See you 'round."

"Not round." She sounded gloomy again. "Here, Jack. If you see me, it'll be here, behind this counter."

"You been grounded?"

Ravi approached. His flashing eyes swiped me as I slipped out past a confused Warren.

Dad came to supper in time to catch my black eye's sunset. Mum had been calm about the plan from the moment he rang to make it. And calmer generally about life for several weeks beforehand. It'd been a while since Tommy had inflated the silver bladder of her last catering sherry box to boot it over the fence. Rosie had removed the kitchen cigarettes without any opposition, and Mum had been enjoying her stove again, abandoning serial chickens in favour of real home cooking.

The evening started well, everyone being very grown up. Mum and Dad even insisted we all splash down the Rhine wine with them and the suddenly tiddly Tommy didn't realise that he was boring us with the commentary on his first-ever-goal-from-an-overhead-kick. When he eventually shut up, I decided to share with them a version of my fight which was, like Tommy's tale, ever-improving.

"*In school*? With *Michael*? So the skip story..."

"... Came in handy, Mum. I didn't expect you to believe it."

"Why didn't you tell me the truth?"

"You'd have rung and..."

"Dead right. And I'll ring Ronaldson tomorrow. And the Head."

"See, I shouldn't have mentioned it."

"What was the fight about?" asked Dad.

"Just a standard power play, Dad."

"And who won?"

"Martin! How can you ask?"

"Don't worry, Mum. No-one really won."

"You mates with Michael again, then?"

"We leave each other alone, Tommy."

"At a respectful distance, is it?"

"Exactamente, Tommy."

"I wish I'd done more of that..." said Dad.

"Of what, Martin?" She poured him another glass.

"Fighting. Do you know, I have never hit anyone? Ever!"

I stroked my dulling shiner.

"Well, personally, I'm glad," Mum said.

"Polly! I mean I have never had a fight with another bloke, have never scrunched a nose, blackened an eye, split a knuckle on a man's face."

"Eeeerrrr! Dad!"

"I would hate to have to do it, Rosie – but I wish I *had done* it."

"'Sall right, you know, a good punch," said Tommy, "I remember when..."

"Warriors, the pair of you!" Mum smiled. "Where did you get it from?"

"Mmm, I wonder, Mum!" said Rosie, clutching her.

"And you're no pussycat, either," she said, straightening Rosie's fingers with their newly glitter-varnished talons.

"I suppose I could clock my boss one, eh Jack? If I could reach across all that distance we must keep! That's why I haven't ever swung one: respectful distance." This rambling told me he was still being highly shat on at the office and I suppose I felt sorry for him.

At last I was offered another glass of wine and we drank to my GCSEs and finished the vegetable bake, moving on to chocolate mousse which I stuck to the roof of my mouth for delicious mixing with the cup of tea which followed. When we moved into the other room and Dad had settled in his usual chair, he suddenly challenged us to remember our most frequent question to him when we were little.

"When are you going to be a millionaire?"

"Wow! That was quick, Rosie. And right."

"And you always said you just needed another tenner," said Tommy.

"So I did!"

"Well, Dad?"

"Rosie, you must have learnt *something* about your old man by now... He is *never* going to be a millionaire. But the reason I mention all this is because I *have* achieved something."

"What?" we cried together.

"I've made it to a million air miles!"

"Oh Martin, you haven't!"

"Well, more or less, Polly."

"More, I should think. I hate – hated – all that travelling so much."

"Well, hang on..."

"Surely they can find younger—"

"No, please, ssshhh. The *point* of all this, Polly – or rather Jack – is that I've decided to make *you* an offer..."

"Me?"

"You! I owe you after all!" They all looked at me. "So this is my offer: *if* you sit through every one of your GCSE exams from beginning to end without bolting, I'll give you a return ticket to visit your friend Dan in New York."

"Oh my God! That's not fair!" Tommy turned to face the wall, asking it to give him strength.

"But doesn't the offer depend on his results?" said Mum. "He's getting quite good at not bunking, you know."

"Then he should be rewarded, shouldn't he? You may or may not know, Polly, but I made a spectacular mess of our last deal. I don't want to take any chances with this one – or with Jack's exams. I believe his results depend on his hanging in there till the bitter end."

"So I just have to attend all my exams. Is that right?"

"Yup. Though obviously I am hoping you will make good use of the time. Mr Finch seems to think you are on target for a good grade in Business Studies."

"New York! I can't believe it."

"Do we have a deal?"

"It's a lovely idea, Martin, so long as the Jackson-Fains can meet his plane."

"A deal, Dad, but can I have it in writing?" No way were a few thousand air miles going to cancel his debt, but he tried and I will always be grateful for that.

I went down to Emporio more and more often. I wouldn't always make it inside, of course, and if Ravi was at the glass door on ruffian-watch I didn't even bother getting off the bus. But I did coincide with some of his absences. And Warren quickly worked out I wasn't coming for any more Eng Lit tips.

I spent more time with Dad during the holidays – or at least more time with his flat. I suppose I was rewarding him for his performance at home. Perhaps I was reduced to making a friend of him. Perhaps I had to, now that I had lost Dan and Michael.

One night he got in before sundown and we went into Hyde Park. We talked as we walked about the family supper and the deal. He was obviously pleased with himself though I felt he still deserved to have it hard.

"You've got what it takes, Jack," he suddenly said. "Do you hear me?"

"What do you mean?"

"In business. I really think you could go far. You know how to get what you want out of people. And you've got a good mind. You're bright and you're resilient."

"What if I don't *want* to go into business?"

"Well, I wouldn't worry about what you want now," he told me as he turned away from the Serpentine Gallery. "If I guarantee you nothing else, Jack, it is that you'll come round to business – probably as soon as you hit the sidewalks of New York."

Back home I was now doing all Mum's shopping for her at Emporio, infuriating Ravi with my ponderous selection, my frequent enquiries of a certain assistant and my tarrying over the new and old titles at the video counter – and all the ones in between. He tried shielding her behind the phalanx of Bollywood and Hollywood cardboard hunks. But they couldn't stop me suggesting a meeting. I wanted to get her out of the area. I wanted to take her to see something artistic, for emotional reasons; and it would have been too emotional to go to one I'd done with Dan.

"Do you know the Serpentine Gallery?" I asked.

"Course not. But I'll find it," she replied.

Then a few weeks into my last compulsory year of education, I lost a wadge of coursework essays. This rocked me profoundly. I valued those essays. They may not have been the best, but they were done, and done in sweat. I was certain Michael was lashing back. To Ronaldson's misplaced delight he had been in school more than usual. Now I knew he had simply been learning my routine, leering at my files, stalking them before the inevitable theft.

Did I have the stomach for another confrontation? Did I have the eye socket, the shin for another fight? I didn't want to give Michael the pleasure. But he would surely submit the essays as his own or, more likely, market them for a wider audience. I imagined myself at the auction, desperately bidding for every copy, determined to recover my intellectual property and Michael, in bow tie and smug good humour, refusing to acknowledge my crazy waving.

"At last you're acting like a normal teenager," Mum

said of my new obsession with security. "We were afraid I was *never* going to be banned from your bedroom."

"Well, you are now."

I flicked through Michael's poxy file when he was sent out of class but I found none of my dense typing amongst his depressing scraps of work and lovingly ill-drawn logos. My remaining files I kept with me at all times, even under my tray in the canteen.

Then suddenly the mocks were in my face – and I was wishing my persecutor still sold cheat-packs. I felt ready for none but English and History, stumbling blindly on the others, rakes thwacking up in my face. I hoped for some sort of Christmas miracle, some immediately empowering New Year's resolution, another new start. I returned to school to hear that I had failed everything except English and Business Studies. To Dad's hysterical gratification, I came top in bloody Business Studies.

Everyone who had sent a good luck card now offered advice. Even Nobbi wanted to add a complimentary couple of pounds' worth of opinion. Ronaldson pointed out that I was in danger of making him look stupid opposite Bumcheeks and gave me a hard time over photosynthesis.

"I can't believe you haven't worked it out yet. It comes up sure as the sun. You are *giving* away marks."

"I can't study something without a soul," I offered.

"That is rubbish." He picked up a passing tennis ball and lobbed it into a nearby group.

"Plants don't have souls so I don't have time for them."

"Pretentious rubbish, Jack. What's so soulful about Business Studies? That's just hustling with jargon. I'm counting on you to show some of your own soul this summer. Not potential. Not effort. But soul. Look, let's go through photosynthesis one more time. See the light, please..."

A plane and then the buzzer drowned him out.

I was revising extremely hard in my room that evening – well, making a multi-coloured revision timetable – when Rosie breached security.

"Out!"

"Why?"

"Working." And not looking up.

"Jack! Please remember, exams aren't everything."

"Please go away, Rosie. Now."

But she didn't.

"You don't respect me, do you, Jack?" she wailed on, pushing it.

"I do!"

"Don't! You can't! Liar!"

"I can! I'm not!"

"Where's the Valentine card I sent you then? You haven't even bothered to put it up. That's how much you respect..."

"I don't know. Here somewhere." I rummaged vigorously, toppling a great pile of stuff inside my wardrobe. "I bet Mum tidied it away before I banned her..." She let me rootle, tapping her foot.

"Ha, so that just *proves* you're a liar. I didn't even *send* you a card this year because you've become so *booooooring*."

"But you did, Rosie. I'm sure I remember seeing it..." More stuff including the luminous Chrysler Tower from Dan slid off my desk and on to the floor. Still I searched, emptying the contents of two drawers until...

"There!" I held the Valentine card up in front of her. "Now do you deny it?"

"Yup." She examined the card. "It wasn't me!"

"It wasn't?"

"I swear."

"But you always..."

"Not this year!"

"Well who... hang on!"

"Who, Jack. Tell me. You're not so boring now. I promise. I'll keep it a secret if you tell me."

I smelt the card. Could I get some Tiptop scent off it? There *was* something there! I was sure anyway. I hugged Rosie, spun her round and round and out of my door.

I kissed the card a few times and then got all graphological about the question mark. Only when I could read nothing more into the nonchalant kink of the main structure and the subject nipple of its punctuating ink did I see, just emerging from my wardrobe chaos, the sheaf, the wadge, the lost essays. I leapt up for double joy, more convinced than ever of Laila's beautiful powers.

I skittered across the park from Dad's flat. Laila was there. We were coinciding with an exhibition of spiky installations by Rebecca Horn. We wandered around separately for a while, and then found ourselves together staring at a pair of great metal arms. Hinged at the base, they moved slowly, mechanically together, apparently intending to complete a circle.

I noticed a small horn near the top of each semi-circle, explained not by the artist's name but by the piece's, which was 'The Kiss of the Rhinoceros'. As the two metal pieces entered kissing distance, a powerful electrical charge leapt from tip to tip. The 'kiss', an urgent, mutual lunge, left the arms quivering from the charge. They had recoiled but began inexorably to close the large gap again. When, after several minutes, it came, I gasped with pleasure.

Laila laughed. We looked at each other. She looked at my mouth and I, being even more specific, fixed my eye on her bottom lip. "Aren't you going to ask how I escaped from all my cardboard gaolers?"

"No."

Suddenly we were hinged, her blue boots on my trainers. Hand in hand we leaned back against each other, counterbalancing. Looking, appraising, okaying, praising. Then in time with the installation we reeled in, our hands creeping up each other's arms, feeling the muscles, almost flexing the bones in our determination not to let go now, not now our fingers were approaching each other's shoulders. Closer, closer, it was bound to happen. As the electricity cracked across Horn's gap, we fell together and kissed. A guard looked disapproving but a group of middle-aged art-lovers applauded our creative response to the installation.

I was at it again. A couple of volts of guilt – more aptly measured as dans – flashed in my eyes, but there was too much else to think about: her lips, her mouth, her tongue, her lips, her mouth, her tongue. Her teeth which now clashed with mine, her hair tangling in my fingers at the back of her head. Her beautiful skull! Which held so much of her and was now held by me. When I opened my eyes on hers which laughed, smiled and seemed to be loving me as much as any rhino, I loved her back.

I got two letters the next morning, the first I opened being from Dan, full of excitement about the news of my forthcoming trip. Guilt struck me again and without Laila to kiss me to distraction it became a painful headache. The other was from Laila herself, saying she couldn't see me, which did nothing for my head. Her dad had come home early and discovered her absence. Now she was ultra-grounded: "I will be six foot under if I go out again," she wrote. "It is best if we do not try to see each other, Jack. Please try to understand."

"What you being miserable about?" Nobbi asked as I kicked the frail tree outside his shop.

"Girlfriend." I felt I could confide.

"Want one?"

"Got one."

"Problem?"

"Cultural."

"Tiptop Ravi's daughter?"

"How d'you know?"

"Rosie."

"I'll..."

"*I'll* thank you for not taking out your frustrations on your lovely little sister. Or my tree."

"Sorry."

"So what's wrong with the love thing?"

"We started going out and now she says she can't see me any more."

"D'you give her that mango?"

"Course."

"I see. And how long did you say you'd been seeing her when she tells you this?"

"One hour."

"Hang in there a while longer, eh? Persevere, Jack. And if she don't want to see you, use the time to frigging revise not kick the sap out of the only council decision I have ever benefited from. All right?"

"All right, Nob." I stroked his new tree.

"Completely buggered the blackbird, this has! Blocked the trajectory of the swoop, innit!"

YOU HAVE TWO MINUTES LEFT. REMEMBER TO CHECK. AND CHECK AGAIN.

By that Monday night, though, I was frantic. I told Mum I would go and do some more food shopping for the week.

"What? More?"

When I reached Emporio Tiptop Laila looked up briefly and scowled.

"What's this?" I asked. The entire counter space usually littered with pictures of passionate beauties kissing their faces off was now taken over with files and books of a GCSE nature, with extra supplies stacked neatly behind Clint Eastwood's cardboard boots.

"Revision, of course. I've started in earnest."

"Fine." I realised I hadn't given my revision timetable a second thought since completing it. In fact I had ignored work utterly.

"I've come about your letter, of course."

She was scribbling notes, apparently from her head in which I now occupied not one synapse. I didn't know what to say. "Where's Warren?"

"Resigned."

"Why?"

"You," she whispered. "And, I suppose, me."

"Really?"

"I told him about our... meeting. He completely freaked. Said he had loved me for eleven weeks or eleven months or something. I'm sorry about my letter but I must warn you I am not going to let our... relationship get in the way of my exams."

"Admirable, Laila, but—"

"And I should also warn you that my father is travelling at speed from the chiller cabinet towards us... So what video were you looking for?"

Ravi's shadow did indeed fall across the video counter before she had completed the threat.

"Pappa," said Laila, voice full of foreboding. "Remember what I told you. Jack is a friend. He is good. He is like Warren. Trustworthy. And he, too, is leaving. Please, Pappa! Do not be aggressive."

Ravi was holding a card – and a little grin.

"I am well aware of Jack's qualities, my dear. I have had them coming at me from all sides. You, Mummy – and just now that formidable rival in fresh produce, Nobbi has been telephoning me. And since the departure of Warren has to be coped with I thought I would offer you the chance to consider this..."

He brandished the card.

"Pappa?"

"Ravi?" Sunita wanted to know what he was up to as badly as Laila.

"I would like to give you – *you*, Jack – first sight of what I have just inked out." He flicked it to and fro and then passed it to me. 'Wanted,' I read, 'Part-time shop assistant – all round duties *excepting* video section.'

"If you would like to take the job I am offering then I will not window display it. I will rip it in two."

"Of course I would like the job, sir." I beamed at Laila and had to note in my quick-eyed beloved that where there should have been joy there was angry opposition.

"Please, it's Ravi, Jack."

We shook hands.

"Can I say something, Pappa?"

"Of course."

"In there please, Pappa." She led the way swiftly into the storeroom.

"It seems he does listen to his wife after all," said Sunita, laying a hand lightly on my arm. "I have finally made him realise you are in no way a ruffian."

"Thank you, Sunita."

"You know when Nobbi called, that was the clincher. Ravi has always hated to be teased about his mouldy vegetables by Nobbi and he was so pleased to be able to discuss something else. And then it was an incidental joy and a relief for him to discover your impeccable retail credentials. Apparently it's hard to beat a Chevy Oak boy."

When they came out Ravi shook my hand again and the adults left us to talk.

Speaking very fast and even shaking upon her stool behind her video counter, Laila told me she was confused. Her father, who had always been so inflexible, had unwittingly added to the confusion by establishing me at the Emporio Tiptop at a time in her precious education when she had to keep the most even keel because she wanted to continue to be a brilliant student and get a scholarship to university which she had to start thinking about right away, so, if I didn't mind, but even if I minded terribly, she would make some rules because it seemed I was going to be around every evening rather than once a fortnight.

"So why has he given me the job?"

"He thinks he will have more control over us if we are both employees."

I tugged Mel Gibson's cardboard sleeve and got him to cover us as I leant across. We enjoyed a long kiss at the end of which I said, "Some hope!"

Not a ruffian, but a bit of a rogue rhino, giving his mate something to think about.

Nevertheless she used her lunch break in her school's computer room to print out a 'Colleagues' Contract' which obliged me to keep myself and my kisser well away from her area until such time as she wanted me. These times included three minutes kissing at the top of every hour, providing of course neither parent was watching. 'Occasional liaisons in the storeroom are to be organised at mutually convenient times and under appropriate pretence of work being done,' ran another key clause. We signed and sealed it appropriately.

After sixty minutes of my first evening I was fit to explode. But I was pleased to see her fist passionately scrunch up a page of algebra as we tussled on the counter. The prospect of round two sustained me through a restocking of the dairy fridge but when, twenty minutes short of time, Ravi left the shop, with Sunita at the till, we dived into the storeroom for topnotch snoggings on the rusty coffin freezer.

Later that week, she appeared to relax even more and in response to my beckoning slipped out from behind her counter to visit me – breaking contract – at breads and biscuits. Later she came over to help unpack a box of noodles. Bottom row shelves we found to be out of the security camera's reach. At her desk I dominoed the cinema hunks with my mid-kiss back-kicks and Laila's jean rivets punctured more than one bag of rice in the storeroom.

One evening, mid-hour, Nobbi burst in and caught me staring at her from behind the tilting carousel of tights.

"What are you *doing*?"

"Nothing. I mean, stripping down this shelf of preserves and giving it a thorough scrubbing."

"You bloody idiot, giving her the sheep's eye treatment when you should be studying. Your teacher is always asking me about you these days. I said I'd come down and check on you. You should be reading, mate, like her. Get the bloody books out. Ravi will never notice."

The thought of he and Ronaldson discussing my future somehow encouraged me to maintain a space for an open textbook on a lower shelf of bottled sauces. The next night I effectively shelved love and began my revision. The books stuck in the gooey debris and I couldn't get comfortable. But as I read more and understood more I found it easier, less sticky. That shelf became a secret desk, my multi-coloured timetable stored for easy reference between packs of porridge.

As Laila had said, a lot of this reading was vision rather than revision, but that at least made it more interesting. Besides there is nothing like looking up from a spurt of concentration and seeing the most beautiful girl in the world and thinking that she might look up too.

Laila started firing me GCSE questions, especially Science and mental Maths while I shifted stuff around the shop. It was communication at least. Besides, she harangued if I refused to answer so it was better to be prepared. Increasingly I was ready, even managing a slick explanation of photosynthesis for Ronaldson when he poked his head into the shop one day.

And so that's how I was prepared for these past three weeks at this desk, scribbling everything I have so recently learnt back out again. I have found a target for most facts, even those which came bouncing in at the very last minute. With just a couple of skidding touches on my memory, they have gone on to hit some answer booklet. And lots of my paragraphs have hitched themselves to each other to form trains of thought, rolling in roughly the same direction. Conclusions have been reached, deductions have been made, with workings out to prove that facts can photosynthesise into coherent answers under my sunny concentration. There have been gaps but they've not been too wide and I've been going fast enough to shoot on over. Let's hope.

PENS DOWN!

NO TALKING. LISTEN TO ALL INSTRUCTIONS.

In a few minutes I'll be off through the gates to celebrate the end of our exams with Laila – if Ravi has let her out. Ronaldson has come in as part of the final invigilating team. I will probably shake his hand. Then I'll go up to the library to say farewell to Schuman. More teachers are filing in. Perhaps they are expecting what Bumcheeks calls 'inappropriate scenes' at the end of our last paper.

I SAID "PENS DOWN!"

That'll be obeyed by many of us for life.

STAY SEATED. BE QUIET.

Mrs Carew smiles at me and squeaks past in the shoes that have pissed us off in every exam. There's Michael and there's Razza, sad Razza, whose efforts to go straight weren't helped by being thick. But at least George has still got a job.

HAVE YOUR ANSWERS READY FOR COLLECTION! MAKE SURE THE COVER SHEET IS FILLED OUT CORRECTLY.

Quick! I mustn't forget that or my result won't be valid. Now, steady. I must do this properly.

Name?

Young Mr Churchill passed his exams up the road in that school in Harrow just by writing his name. Let's hope they've tightened up on the marking. I've got to sign this paper, this one more than any.

Exam number?

2-4-6-8, it's never too late – to make a point:

I hereby dedicate my Business Studies GCSE to my father.

I don't need it because, Dad, I'm the business.

Laila and New York, here I come.